OFF ON AN ADVENTURE

The Story of a Girl

D.M. ROSE

ISBN 978-1-64670-343-2 (Paperback)
ISBN 978-1-64670-344-9 (Hardcover)
ISBN 978-1-64670-345-6 (Digital)

Covenant Books, Inc.
11661 Hwy 707
Murrells Inlet, SC 29576
www.covenantbooks.com

For my parents: Thanks for always encouraging
me to use my imagination.

What sort of things do you imagine?

Mermaids? Fairies? Princes and princesses? Sword-fighting pirates? Sailing the vast ocean on a grand ship and seeing far-off lands? All those things were an average adventure for thirteen-year-old Ruthella Blake.

What if the things you imagined weren't just in your imagination though? Impossible you say? I hardly think so! When Ruthella comes face to face with her imagination in the real world, she learns that imagination can sometimes turn into a reality!

Logic will get you from A to B. Imagination
will take you everywhere.
—Albert Einstein

C O N T E N T S

CHAPTER 1

Ella

They say that all great stories start out with, "Once Upon A Time." So why should this story be any different? So here we go—once upon a time, far away, depending on where you live, of course, in a land called Missouri, there lived a girl. Her name was Ruthella Blake. Everyone called her Ella though.

Ella was an average girl of thirteen, with shoulder-length brown hair, brownish-green eyes, and a *big* imagination! She lived in a cozy neighborhood with her parents, right outside the small town of Rocheport. Of course, Ella didn't stay there very long. But we'll get into that soon.

As Ella sat on the bus watching the raindrops dribble down the windowpane, she reflected on her day at school. During third period, Chip Daniels threw an eraser at Charlie Conner, but misaimed and hit Ella by mistake. On her way to math class, Ella saw a couple of younger kids being picked on and went over to help them. The younger kids were very grateful that Ella stood up for them. At lunch, someone running by hit the table Ella was sitting at and knocked a cup of water over on to Ella's notebook and almost ruined her history notes.

"Hmm…" Ella mumbled to herself. "It's been a rough day. I need to get out of here."

As the bus slowed to a halt at Ella's street corner, Ella saw her mom waving to her as she made her way off the bus.

Ella's mother, Emily, was a lovely woman with brown hair and brown eyes. Her smile could light up a room, and it always seemed to make things all right.

"How was school?" asked Emily.

"Long and dangerous," Ella replied.

"Dangerous? What happened?" Emily asked. As the two of them walked hand in hand down the street, Ella told her mom about everything that happened that day.

"I'm very proud of you for standing up for those younger kids. And your notes didn't get ruined, so that's good. I think your day went better than you think it did," Emily smiled.

"Yeah, I guess so, but…" Ella smiled up at her mom. Emily smiled back at her daughter, knowing exactly what she was thinking.

"Adventure time? Where to today?" she asked. Smiling, Ella thought for a minute.

"Hmm… Maybe I'll visit the duchess. Oh! Or perhaps the fairy queen," Ella replied, finally.

"What about the Master of Arms?" Emily asked. "I'm sure he would love to hear about your heroics today."

"Hmm… That's a thought. I haven't gone to visit Harold for a while," Ella mentioned. The two continued down the street to their house and soon heard the familiar honking of a car horn.

"Daddy!" Ella shouted with happiness as she waved to her father, who was waving back at her and his wife.

Ella's dad, Allan, was a cheerful man that almost always had a smile on his face. With his strawberry blond hair and green eyes, you would almost think that you were looking at a leprechaun.

"Well, if it isn't the two most beautiful girls in the world! How did I get so blessed?" Allan asked as he walked over to them. Emily beamed a big bright smile and flushed a bit red like she wasn't at all used to hearing her husband compliment her. Allan flashed her an ornery smile before kissing her.

"Daddy, you're embarrassing Mommy!" Ella stated, turning a little pink herself. Allan laughed and kissed his daughter's head.

"I don't think Mommy is the only one that's turning a bit red," he winked.

Ella couldn't deny it; her father's wonderfully sincere compliments were great, and they made her feel special.

"So, what are my lovely girls up to today?" Allan asked as they were strolling up the walkway.

"We were just discussing Ella's next adventure," Emily answered.

"Oh! Where are you off to this time? How about ancient Rome or the old west?" Allan asked.

"Hmm… Maybe, but I was thinking about going to see Harold," Ella answered.

"The Master of Arms?" Allan asked.

"Yeah. I haven't gone to see him in a while," Ella commented.

"Harold is a good one to visit. What about the admiral though?" Allan asked. "I haven't heard you mention him for a good while either."

"The admiral! Good old Arny!" Ella exclaimed. "I haven't gone to see him in a long time! That's the perfect idea, Daddy! I need to get going before it gets dark. Love you both, and be home by dinnertime, okay?" she said to her parents as she ran off with her backpack.

"What about your homework?" Emily yelled.

"I'll have the admiral, or his sergeant help me with it. I promise I'll have it done when I get home," Ella yelled back with a smile.

Ella's parents beamed with pride for their daughter as they watched her run *off on an adventure*.

Ella loved her backyard; it was fenced in all the way around, and her mother had planted flowers everywhere. Growing near the end of the yard was a large oak tree that had to be at least one hundred years old, but was still very strong and sturdy. Allan had once started to build a treehouse up in the old oak tree, but upon finishing the platform, Ella asked him to leave it as is. She claimed that she could see the whole world from that platform, and a treehouse would only get in the way. So Allan put in some railing and secured a ladder to it. That platform was where Ella left on all of her adventures.

Ella climbed up the ladder of the old oak tree and sat on the platform with her back against the trunk of the tree and her backpack in her lap to be sure she didn't forget it. As Ella listened to the sounds of nature, she closed her eyes. When she opened them again, she was on the docks of a massive port near a huge ship called *The Fair Maiden*, and the ship was ready to set sail.

"I better hurry!" Ella said to herself as she picked up the skirt of her period accurate dress and started to run up the platform to board the ship.

"Halt! Sorry, little miss, no maidens allowed on deck!" said a foreman.

Ironic, isn't it? A ship called *The Fair Maiden* and no maidens allowed on board. Go figure.

"I'm here to see Admiral Arnold Cloak. Mention that Lady Ruthella is here, and I'm sure he'll make an exception," Ella told the foreman. "And please hurry, the ship is ready to depart."

"Yes, madam. I wouldn't hold your breath though, little miss. The admiral is strict with these rules," answered the foreman.

Ella smiled as the foreman walked to the admiral's cabin; a few minutes later returning with the admiral.

The admiral was an older gentleman in his late seventies. He had white hair and a white square cut beard with a kind face. He was beaming from ear to ear when he saw Ella.

"Lady Ruthella, the Jewel of the Sea! I haven't seen you in ages! It is my sincerest pleasure to welcome you aboard," he said, bowing to her. Ella smiled up at the admiral and gave him a hug.

"Hello, Arny! I've missed you and this lovely ship of yours," she stated as she looked around the beautiful ship.

"You flatterer," Arny laughed. "It is wonderful to see you, my dear."

Ella smiled and held the admiral's hand as the two of them walked to the side railing. The sea air smelled so crisp. The cool mist brushed the hair away from Ella's face, and the sound of the waves lapping against the side of the ship was so relaxing. A day at sea was just the ticket!

"So, my dear, what brings you here today?" asked the admiral.

Ella told the admiral of the day's happenings as she watched gulls fly close to the water searching for fish.

"It sounds like you had a very fair day!" the admiral stated. All Ella could do was smile; even if it was a terrible day at sea, the admiral always found something good in it.

"I suppose you're right," she replied. "Oh! Arny, would you or the sergeant be able to help me with my homework?" she asked. "I just need someone to check my final answers when I'm done."

"I'm sorry, my dear, I have to oversee the ship today because Barnabas went a day ahead of us to make staying arrangements for myself and the crew at Port Berg," Arny answered. Ella's face saddened a bit, but she nodded her understanding.

"Ah! Perhaps my new cabin boy could assist you and check your work though?" he suggested.

"That sounds all right. When did he come aboard?" she asked.

"Oh, about a week or so ago. He's a hard worker and always incredibly honest," replied the admiral.

"He sounds like a good member for the crew," Ella complimented.

"He is. Antonio! Come here, lad!" Arny called.

"Yes, sir!" Antonio answered as he started walking over.

Antonio was a very handsome young man that looked to be about fifteen. He had short layers of brown-blond hair and bangs that hung in his face. He had very deep brown eyes with flecks of hazel and tanned skin that made it nearly impossible to see the small sprinkling of freckles across his nose.

He looks so young! Ella thought to herself. *He couldn't be much older than me!*

"Yes, sir? How may I serve you, Admiral?" Antonio asked.

"Antonio, I'd like to introduce you to Lady Ruthella. Lady Ella is the Jewel of the Sea and the only exception to my rule!" Arny explained as he introduced Ella, making her smile.

Antonio bowed and took Ella's hand to kiss it.

"My lady," he said formally.

Ella's face turned bright red! No boy had ever kissed her hand before. She somehow managed a tiny smile behind her red face though.

"I relieve you of your duties for the time being. If you wouldn't mind, you are to help Lady Ella with her homework," ordered the admiral. "Is this acceptable for both parties?" he asked.

"Of course, sir," Antonio replied. Still a bit pink, Ella gave a shy nod.

"Good! Off you go then!" Arny commanded.

Ella picked up her backpack and walked to the upper deck of the ship where they kept huge rolls of rope that Ella could fit inside. She plopped her bag into one of the rope coils and then slid in herself. Antonio had followed Ella to the upper deck and watched curiously as she climbed into the ropes. He walked over and peeked in at Ella, who was already in her book.

She glanced over the top of her history book and said, "Hello."

"Hi," Antonio laughed.

"Is there something I can help you with?" she asked.

"Am I not the one that's supposed to be helping you?" he asked.

"I'm fine doing the work alone," she answered. "I just need someone to check my final answers."

"The admiral told me to help you, and I won't let him down. So I shall wait," he stated as he sat staring while Ella tried to get back to reading.

Wow, he thought to himself as he stared at her. Ella glanced over the top of her book a few seconds later, and Antonio was still staring.

"Ugh! It's really hard to concentrate with you staring at me!" she complained.

"Sorry. What am I supposed to do though?" he asked.

"I don't know. Don't you have duties on the ship?" she asked.

"The admiral relieved me of my duties so I could help you. So, I have nothing to do at the moment," he answered.

"Well, may I relieve you of helping me until I come find you?" she asked.

"As you wish, my lady. Until you require my assistance, I shall return to my duties," he replied bowing and then returned to the lower decks.

14

About an hour later, Ella had almost finished her questions and was ready to be back on the lower decks where she could watch the crew and deckhands with the admiral.

One thing that Ella absolutely loved about visiting Arny were his stories. The admiral would tell Ella stories of him sword fighting on the high seas and about seeing new lands when he was a young cabin boy like Antonio. Thinking of the admiral's stories, Ella didn't realize that Antonio had come to see if she was finished.

"Oh!" she jumped, not expecting to see anyone there.

Laughing, Antonio apologized for scaring her.

"Are you ready for me to check your work?" he asked.

"Yes. Here you go," she replied as she handed him the papers.

"Good penmanship. That's very important," he complimented as he finished checking Ella's work. "All your answers are correct and in order. Well done!"

"Thank you!" she replied as she started to climb out of the ropes.

"Here, allow me, my lady," he said as he easily lifted Ella out.

"Thank you again," she said shyly.

"No trouble at all," he replied.

Ella smiled and made her way back to the main deck to find the admiral.

"All finished, my dear?" Arny asked when he saw Ella approaching.

"Yes, sir!" she answered with a salute. Arny saluted back as he laughed.

"When will we make port, Admiral?" she asked.

"Around dinnertime, I suppose. Will you join us?" he asked.

"I wish I could, but I'll have to head home when we make port," she replied. "Sorry, Admiral."

"Oh, that's all right, my dear. Perhaps you will be visiting a bit more often?" the admiral asked.

Of all the places and people Ella visited, the admiral and his ship were near, if not on the very top of her list of favorites.

"I will try, Arny, but you know how far my adventures take me sometimes," she said with a bit of sadness.

Right as the admiral was going to speak, someone yelled out, "Land dead ahead! Port Berg!"

The admiral's face saddened until he realized that Ella was watching him, so he smiled at her. Ella felt the sad pain in her heart that she always felt when it was nearly time for her to go. She tried to ignore it as she and the admiral stood at the bow of the ship overseeing the crew as they brought *The Fair Maiden* into port.

"Don't let that line slag!" a deckhand yelled.

"Make sure that rope is tight!" yelled a crew member.

The ship always got a lot louder when it made port or during a storm.

When the ship finally docked, Ella gathered up her things.

"You are always welcome on this ship, Lady Ella," Arny stated as he patted her head.

Feeling the goodbye tears start to well up inside, Ella hugged the admiral and said farewell to the crew.

As Ella walked down the docks, she heard someone yell farewell. Turning to see who had yelled, she saw Antonio waving as he smiled at her. Ella waved back and managed a smile with tears running down her cheeks.

A little way off the docks, Ella sat in a patch of grass still crying a bit as she listened to the sounds around her and closed her eyes.

Drip! A drop of rain from one of the leaves above plopped onto Ella's nose. Ella opened her eyes to the drop of rain, and she was back in Missouri. Back in her little neighborhood, and back on the platform up in her tree about to be rained upon by the gray skies that seemed to linger that day. Ella sighed as she picked up her stuff and went inside for dinner.

Emily was busy straining some veggies when Ella walked in.

"Hi, sweetie, how's the admiral?" she asked.

"He's good. He has a new cabin boy. His name is Antonio. He's nice. Arny wants me to visit more often. He misses me," Ella replied.

"That's not surprising. I would certainly miss you. So, is this boy Antonio cute?" Emily asked.

"Mom!" Ella shrieked.

"What? I'm just asking," Emily countered with a wink. Ella's face turned a new shade of red, and Emily noticed.

"Ah, so he is cute! Tell me about him," Emily demanded.

"Mom! He's nice. Arny says he's a hard worker and always incredibly honest. He checked my homework and said that I had good penmanship. He helped me out of the big rolls of rope and kissed my hand when he met me," she answered, her face possibly even redder.

"Well, it sounds like he's quite the gentleman! If Arny wants you to visit more, this young man sounds like a good reason to," Emily teased. Ella rolled her eyes and sat down at the table. Emily was still giggling as she took dinner out of the oven.

"Well, look who's back! How's the admiral doing? And who is this new cabin boy I was overhearing about?" Allan asked as he came into the kitchen. Ella sank in her chair.

"Oh, I've heard all about him! I'll catch you up later!" Emily winked at her husband. Allan grinned and returned the wink.

"Can we talk about a different part of my adventure, please?" Ella asked, her face still pink.

"We're just teasing, sweetie!" Emily assured her. "Tell us about the rest of your trip."

As Ella told her parents about her adventure, they were smiling.

"I cried when I had to say goodbye though. I really should visit Arny more. He's a wonderful man, and he tells the best stories," Ella concluded.

"That's a good idea. The admiral is an honorable man," Allan stated.

"Do you think you'll go see him again tomorrow?" Emily asked. Ella thought about it for a while, slightly playing with her food.

"That hard to decide, huh?" Allan asked.

"It really is! I have so many adventures and places to go, and so many people that I can visit! How can I possibly choose to only go on one adventure and only visit one of the amazing people I know?" Ella asked, frowning.

"It's all up to you, my dear adventurer. We've always told you to let your imagination take you wherever you want to go. Sometimes your heart will tell you where you *really* want to be though," Allan told his daughter.

"And sometimes all you have to do is listen," Emily winked.

Ella smiled at her parents, they always knew how to make her feel better and encourage her.

"Can I be excused, please?" Ella asked with a hopeful grin. "I think I might have time for one more adventure."

"Not tonight, sweetie. It's dark and raining. You should save your adventure for tomorrow. It is Saturday, so you'll have the entire day to adventure and be in your imagination. With so many places to visit, who knows where you may end up," Emily pointed out.

"I forgot that tomorrow was Saturday! This is why you're so smart, Mommy," Ella stated.

CHAPTER 2

....

Swords and Confusion

Ella woke up early the next morning and after searching for the cereal and having no success in finding it, she sat in the kitchen watching the sun come up.

A few minutes later, Emily came into the kitchen rubbing her eyes.

"Good morning, little sunshine," she yawned. "You're up before the sun!"

"Yeah, I don't want to waste any time. Can I please have my breakfast so I can go?" Ella asked.

"I'm surprised you haven't eaten already," Emily remarked.

"I couldn't find the cereal," Ella replied.

"That's because your dad put it away. I haven't been able to find it either," Emily mumbled as she opened cabinets trying to find the cereal her husband put, God only knows where.

Allan came in the kitchen and hugged his wife, not really noticing her search.

"Good morning, my dears," Allan said cheerfully.

"Morning," Emily mumbled, still involved in her search.

"Honey, what are you looking for?" he asked.

"The cereal! No one can find it! Where in the world did you put it?" Emily asked with an exasperated expression.

Allan walked over to a cabinet that Emily had checked, at least five times before with no success, and pulled out a box of cereal.

"Right here," he answered. Ella watched as her mother's face fell.

"I looked in that cabinet though!" Emily stated in a frustrated tone.

Ella couldn't help giggling at her mother's frustration. This wasn't the first time Allan had put something in a place only he could find. Emily snatched the box of cereal out of her husband's hand and put it on the counter.

"You okay, hon?" Allan asked, innocently.

Emily playfully glared at her husband, but couldn't help laughing at his innocent yet ornery face.

"What am I going to do with you?" she sighed as she hugged her husband.

Ella smiled at how cute she thought her parents were together.

After, Emily got Ella a bowl for her cereal; Ella ate fast and put her bowl in the sink.

"I'm off on my adventure!" Ella stated as she headed out the back door in the kitchen.

Ella climbed up the ladder to her platform and sat down with her back against the trunk. She watched the pink and orange morning clouds move across the sky for a minute before closing her eyes.

Suddenly, the early birds weren't singing anymore. Instead, she heard the sounds of swords clashing together. When Ella opened her eyes, she saw the playful duel of two shipmate pirates having a grand old time. She smiled and stood up to join the rest of the crew to watch.

"Who's winning?" Ella whispered.

"Toni," answered one of the shipmates.

"Ah," she breathed. "Which one is Toni?" she asked.

"The one that's winning!" answered the seemingly annoyed shipmate.

Thank you, Captain Obvious. I doubt you're a captain though, Ella thought to herself. *Hmm… He looks really familiar. Toni that is, not Captain Obvious.*

Toni gracefully disarmed his opponent an instant later. Normally you would see a blade to the loser's throat, but Toni went and picked up the sword and tried to hand it back to his opponent. The crew and shipmates started booing and scoffing. They clearly didn't approve. Toni's opponent wouldn't accept the sword that was being offered either and held up his hands in surrender.

"What? You will simply give up so easily?" Toni breathlessly asked his opponent, who nodded.

Toni shrugged with disappointment and eyed the shipmates and crew looking for his next opponent. He searched the crowd until his eyes landed on Ella.

"You," Toni said, pointing at Ella and beckoning for her to get a sword.

Ella's eyes grew wide as she stood motionless, unsure of what she should do. Although the admiral and the Master of Arms had taught Ella a few things in the past, she had never actually fought anyone before. And at that moment, she couldn't remember a single thing she had learned!

"Hey, come on," Toni said a bit louder.

"Aye, wench!" shouted the crew member next to Ella as he pushed her to get her attention. "The—"

"ENOUGH!" Toni boomed.

All eyes were on Toni as he started walking over to the crew member, sword still in hand.

Does he just look angry or does he look like he's about to kill someone? Ella thought nervously. *Oh, Lord, I can't tell! I can't watch him kill a man! What do I do?*

Ella's mind was racing as Toni gently moved her aside and pointed his blade at the crew member.

"You will respect the fair maiden aboard this ship. Is that understood?" Toni shouted. The crew member nodded nervously.

"Y-yes, Captain," he stuttered.

"Good!" Toni replied sharply as he lowered his blade and turned to Ella.

"Now, fair maiden, are you all right?" he asked.

Ella nodded.

"Good. Pick up a sword," he demanded.

Okay, so he defends me and now he wants to fight me? I guess in all fairness he did want to fight me before that man said anything, Ella thought quietly to herself as she picked up a sword, hoping she would remember what she had learned.

Toni put his blade up and put his other hand behind his back as he took his stance. Ella briefly looked around for some possible way out of this, but all she could see were the shipmates and crew members laughing at her!

"This is disarm fighting," Toni told her. "Shall we begin?"

What an ornery little smirk! Ella thought to herself, a bit annoyed as she looked at his face. *Those eyes. Gosh, he looks so familiar! How? Or why, I guess.*

Ella was so completely focused on trying to figure out why Toni looked so familiar that she was just standing there staring at him.

"How do I know you?" she asked out loud without realizing. Toni came off guard and looked at Ella with a big ornery smile on his face.

"Captain Antonio Carter, at your service, my lady," Antonio said as he took off his hat and bowed.

"But right now, I am simply your opponent," he stated as he put his hat back on and took his stance once again. "Now pick up your blade and fight me! Show me what you've learned," he winked.

Ella's jaw practically hit the deck!

Antonio? But, Antonio is the admiral's cabin boy! He can't be a pirate captain! Can he? Ella thought to herself with her mouth still hanging open like a cod fish.

"Come on, Ella, pick up your blade. I am growing impatient," Antonio remarked as he took off his hat again to push back his bangs.

It really is Antonio! How is this possible though? Ella's mind was going wild. Antonio rolled his eyes and smiled at Ella.

"I know you can fight, even if you can't remember. I'll go easy on you for now," he whispered. "Now, come on!" he bellowed pretending that his patience had run out.

As Ella finally came out of shock, she lifted her blade and took her stance.

"At last!" he shouted as if he had been waiting a lifetime. "Now we shall have ourselves a good show, lads!"

The crew laughed.

Ella was annoyed by that last statement and decided that she was going to win just so the crew would indeed have a good show.

"Are you ready?" she asked impatiently.

Toni nodded, and the fight was on!

Cling! Clang! Went the swords as Ella and Toni fought. After playing with him for a bit, Ella started to get bored and skillfully disarmed Toni and lowered her blade as she smiled.

Toni looked over at his sword and then back at Ella. He was out of breath, but smiling. The crew was in shock though. Evidently, Toni wasn't one for losing a fight. Ella looked at the crew then back at Toni. She couldn't stop smiling; beating the captain was quite an accomplishment.

"Well done," Toni complimented.

"Thank you!" Ella replied.

"Shall we go again?" he asked. "I won't let you win this time."

"Oh, you *let* me win, did you?" she asked sarcastically.

"You're good, but not that good yet. Go again?" he asked with that ornery smile of his.

Ella ran over and got Toni's sword and handed it back to him.

"No kid stuff this time. Fight for real, and we'll see who the best is!" she stated.

"Agreed," he replied.

Whoa! Ella thought as Toni's blade flew by her head.

Cling! Their blades hit. *Clang!*

Ella did find that she had to duck a lot more in this fight.

Maybe he was taking it easy on me! she thought as she barely missed Toni's cut.

A few parries and dodges later, Ella moved one way, and at the last second without her noticing, Toni's blade went in the other direction and cut her on the arm.

"Ah!" Ella cried out in pain as she dropped her sword.

Toni dropped his sword and ran over to Ella, who was holding her arm to stop the bleeding.

"Okay, you win," she stated.

"That's not how I win. I swear I didn't mean to do that! Are you okay?" he asked.

"I'll be fine. It's just a slash," she answered, checking it over.

Toni ripped a piece of cloth from his shirt and tied it around Ella's arm where she was cut.

"I was hoping this wouldn't happen. Sorry, again," he frowned.

Ella stared at Toni as he hung his head. He looked so remorseful about what he had done, and without being able to control herself, Ella burst out laughing!

"What are you laughing at?" he asked.

"Your face! You look so upset, and I'm the one that's hurt!" she replied as she laughed even harder.

Toni shook his head and rolled his eyes.

"You're insane, you know that?" he asked. He couldn't help smiling as he helped Ella to her feet though.

"If I don't laugh, I'll cry. And besides, laughter is the best medicine," she told him.

Toni gave Ella a playful push before turning to his crew.

"All right, lads, fun's over. Back to work," he ordered as he started to walk away.

"Antonio!" Ella called.

Toni turned around and looked at her.

"Thanks," she said as she pointed to the cloth that bandaged her arm. Toni smiled and continued on his way. Ella watched him for a minute and then turned to go find something to do.

"Ella!" someone yelled. Ella whirled around to look for who called her.

"Ella!" Toni yelled again. Ella gave Toni a puzzled look as he beckoned her over.

"What?" she asked when she reached him.

"You're welcome," he answered.

"Ugh! Did you honestly call me all the way over here for that?!" she asked, sounding frustrated.

"You know, you're cute when you're frustrated. And yes, I did call you all the way over here for that," he laughed.

Ella shot him a dirty look and walked off.

"Oh, come on now, don't walk away mad," he said as he grabbed Ella's hand. Ella pulled her hand away and folded her arms.

"I still don't understand how you're here. You're supposed to be with the admiral! You're supposed to be a cabin boy on *The Fair Maiden*! You're not supposed to be a pirate captain! Why are you a pirate captain?" she asked in one big rush.

Toni stared at Ella for a minute.

"Why don't you tell me?" he asked.

"Don't you know?" she asked.

"Not as well as you should," he replied as he walked off.

"If I knew, I wouldn't be asking," she stated.

"It was your idea. I just went with it," he told her before starting toward the upper deck.

Ella was so confused! Why didn't she remember any of this? Did something happen with the admiral or *The Fair Maiden*? Ella needed answers.

"I have to go see the admiral," she declared to herself as she sat down on a barrel and closed her eyes. A second later, Ella felt a tap on her shoulder and opened her eyes to see who it was.

"Antonio?" she questioned as she looked around.

"Yes. The admiral is looking for you. He's down on the lower deck," he told her.

"So, this is the admiral's ship, right? *The Fair Maiden* is the ship we are currently on?" she asked, sounding a bit unsure.

Antonio gave her a strange look.

"Of course. What other ship would we be on?" he asked.

"Your pirate ship. That's where we were," she answered.

Antonio raised his eyebrow.

"My pirate ship?" he asked, looking confused.

"Yes, but I've yet to find out why you have a pirate ship. Excuse me," she said as she pushed past him to go find Arny.

"Ah! There you are, my dear," Arny said. "I'm so happy you could be here today. I would have been so upset if I didn't get the chance to say goodbye."

Ella's face fell.

"Goodbye? What do you mean goodbye? Where are you going?" she asked.

"I love the sea, my dear, but there is something that I love far more," he told her.

"What?" she asked.

"My wife," he replied.

Ella thought about her father for a minute; about how he was always telling her mother how much he loved her more than anything else in the world (except for Ella, of course), and Ella's heart felt sad.

Arny lifted Ella's chin and said, "Daring adventures are yours to command, and yet you hang your head while you feel this is out of your control. I am happy with this, Lady Ella! It is what I wanted, and you knew."

Ella tried not to, but she started to cry.

"My dear," Arny said as he pulled her into a hug. "Do not cry for me, Lady Ella. You must find a new adventure now and be happy when you do. I cannot bear my last memory of the Jewel of the Sea to be crying. Perk up, my dear. I will never truly be gone from you."

He smiled down at her, and she tried her hardest to put on a brave face. She even managed a smile through the tears.

As the crew gathered on the main deck, Arny addressed them for the last time and dismissed them on good terms. Ella held her head high and suppressed the tears. The entire crew, including Ella, saluted the admiral, and Arny saluted his crew in return. When it was time for Arny to depart from the ship, Ella wrapped him in one last hug.

"I will never be gone from you, my dear. Call on me anytime," Arny told her as he gave her a final squeeze.

When the admiral and the rest of the crew had left the ship, Ella didn't know exactly what she should do.

"This is the last time I'll be on *The Fair Maiden*. I don't want to leave yet," Ella said to herself as she walked over to the railing.

"Why did I end this adventure? I have the ability to make it last forever, so why end it?" she asked herself as she leaned on the ship's railing, watching some gulls.

"Will I ever see you again?" asked a familiar voice.

Ella turned to see Antonio.

"Yes, you will see me again," she answered.

"That's nice to know. What were you saying earlier about a pirate ship?" he asked.

"You will be a great pirate captain and a master swordsman. See? You did this," she said as she lifted her sleeve to reveal the bloodied bandage where she was cut.

"No, I would never hurt the Jewel of the Sea," he stated.

"It was an accident. You moved one way, and I moved the wrong way," she told him.

"Sorry in advance then," he replied.

Ella smiled thinking about Antonio's face when it happened.

"Oh, that's why you said sorry again! You already said it in advance. Okay, I'm starting to understand now," she blurted out.

"What are you talking about?" he questioned.

"Nothing. It's not that important," she answered.

The two of them stood in silence for a minute listening to the sound of the waves crashing.

"Ella?" Antonio said.

"Yes?" she answered.

"Why a pirate?" he asked

Ella started laughing.

"I don't know. I guess you just seem like you would make a good pirate, and you do," she stated with a grin.

Antonio laughed and said, "Okay. If you say so."

"Well, I guess you wouldn't be if I didn't say so," she smarted. She finally understood what Antonio meant by it being her idea for him to be a pirate.

Antonio looked as if he was thinking about something, and right when Ella was about to ask, Antonio blurted out, "Got it!"

"Got what?" she asked.

"I was trying to think of what I will call my pirate ship, but I know now," he answered rather vague.

"What are you going to call it?" she asked.

Antonio shot her that ornery grin of his and said, "You'll find out."

"Fine, I can be patient. I'll find out sooner or later," she stated in a matter-of-fact manner.

The two of them watched the ocean with dreamy eyes while the mist and sea air played with their hair as they stood in silence.

"Ella," someone whispered. Ella looked at Antonio.

"Did you say something?" she asked.

"No," he replied.

"Ella," whispered the voice. From out of nowhere, Ella suddenly felt shoved and hit the side of the ship with a thud!

"Are you okay?" Antonio asked.

"Ella!" whispered the voice again.

"Oof!" Ella blurted out as she smacked into the ship again.

"Ella, stop, you're going to hurt yourself!" Antonio said as he tried to hold onto her.

"It's not me! Oof!" she grunted as she slipped out of Antonio's grip and hit the ship again.

"Ella!" the voice yelled.

"Can you hear that?" Ella asked, looking around.

"Hear what? All I can hear is the thud you're making when you hit the ship," Antonio stated as he held Ella's shoulders.

"Ella!" yelled the voice as Ella hit the ship so hard she was almost thrown overboard.

"Ouch!" Ella shouted.

Antonio tried to grab Ella, but his hands went right through her. Ella and Antonio stared at each other with wide eyes.

"ELLA!" the voice boomed.

Ella got ready for the pain she knew she was about to feel, either from the ship or the icy water, and closed her eyes.

"Ella! Come back!" the voice said, sounding more familiar now. Ella opened her eyes.

"Jenny!" she yelled.

CHAPTER 3

So Says the Captain

"Sorry if I made you hit anything, and I'm really sorry if I have the worst timing ever, but I had to get you back here," Jenny stated.

Ella jumped up and hugged her friend.

Jenny had been Ella's best friend since they were in kindergarten, and the two of them would spend entire days going on adventures together.

A few years ago though, Jenny and her family had to move away because of her dad's job.

Jenny was fourteen, a year older than Ella, with long, blonde, curly hair and hazel eyes with flecks of blue in them.

"You're here! How? Why?" Ella asked in a big rush of excitement.

"A business trip. And thanks to your parents, I get to stay with you all weekend!" Jenny told her excitedly.

"Yes! Okay, you're forgiven for slamming me into the side of a ship," Ella winked.

"Oh! The high seas! This ship, it calls to me. Ella, take me there!" Jenny demanded.

All of Ella's happy feelings suddenly drained away when she remembered that it was the last time she would be on *The Fair Maiden*.

"What's wrong, Ella?" Jenny asked.

I have to find a new adventure and be happy. I can't let Arny down! Ella thought to herself.

"Ella?" Jenny questioned.

"I have a better adventure to show you! It's on a pirate ship, and I happen to know the captain from when he was just a cabin boy," Ella told her.

"Oh, you have me intrigued. Let's go!" Jenny shouted, getting excited.

Ella and Jenny sat down next to the tree trunk and held hands so both of them could go on the same adventure.

"Ready?" Ella asked.

"Let's go!" Jenny answered.

The two of them then closed their eyes.

"Ouch!" Jenny shouted.

Ella opened her eyes and saw that Jenny's hair had gotten whipped across her face by the sea air.

"Are you okay?" Ella asked, laughing.

Jenny blew the hair out of her face and said, "Yeah, I'm fine. I always forget to imagine my hair in an updo when we go out to sea."

"Come on, I want you to meet Antonio," Ella stated as she stood up.

"Antonio? Why does that name sound so familiar?" Jenny asked as she stood up too.

"I don't know. He just came around yesterday for me," Ella replied.

"Hmm…" Jenny murmured as she and Ella walked.

"There he is. Antonio!" Ella yelled.

Toni smiled and waved from the upper deck.

"That's Antonio. Everyone here calls him Toni though," Ella told Jenny.

Jenny stared at Antonio as he came down to the main deck where they were.

"The Jewel of the Sea has returned and brought along another. Welcome aboard, ladies!" he greeted with a bow.

"Do you have a brother?" Jenny asked.

"I have two actually. Why?" he asked.

"Hmm… You just seem familiar," Jenny stated.

Toni just shrugged his shoulders.

"So, where are we sailing to?" Ella asked.

"Mermaid Cove. Rumor has it that at this time every year, the mermaids come up on the rocks and return the lost loot that went down when ships sank," Toni answered.

Ella and Jenny looked at each other with raised eyebrows. They had known their fair share of mermaids. One thing that all mermaids had in common, no matter how nice they were, mermaids did *not* share their treasures!

"Don't go!" Ella and Jenny shouted together.

Toni laughed.

"Did you two practice that?" he asked.

"No. Antonio, something is up! Mermaids don't share their treasures!" Ella told him.

"Yeah, we've known quite a few mermaids and no matter how nice the nicest mermaid is, no mermaid will ever share her treasure. It would be a *big* mistake to go there," Jenny explained.

Toni looked back and forth between the two of them for a minute; carefully thinking about what they had just told him.

"So be it. Set a new course for the nearest trading post," Toni told his first mate with a reluctant look on his face.

"But, Captain…" the first mate protested.

"Just do it," Toni ordered.

"Aye, aye," the first mate obeyed. "So says the captain."

Toni nodded and turned to walk away. He had a sorrowful look on his face as he did though.

"We know mermaids, Toni. So this has got to be some kind of trick," Jenny stated.

Toni put up his hand to show that he had heard enough.

"Antonio, are you okay?" Ella asked as she and Jenny tried to catch up.

"No. There are things you don't know," he stated as he walked into his cabin with the girls following.

"Antonio…" Ella started to say.

"Ella, I don't want to raise my voice at either of you, so please," he said as he waved them off.

Ella and Jenny reluctantly returned to the main deck and overheard some of the men talking.

"I can't believe the captain would do this to Phillip," said one of the men.

"I know. Even after promisin' 'im that 'e'd do anything to get 'is mums ring back so's 'e could marry 'is sweetheart. Aye! You two little wenches got a listenin' problem?" shouted the other man.

"No, we hear just fine," Jenny stated.

"Then 'ear this. Mind yer own!" he shouted.

When he turned around, Jenny stuck her tongue out at him, and Ella couldn't help giggling.

"That must be what Antonio meant by 'things we don't know.' He was going to Mermaid Cove to get Phillip his mother's ring. How did the mermaids get it, though?" Ella asked.

"Yeah, I don't know..." Jenny trailed off.

Ella opened her mouth to say something, but before she could, Jenny burst out, "I've got an idea!"

"Okay. What's your idea?" Ella asked.

A mischievous smile crept onto Jenny's face.

"Let's go find out what Phillip's mom's ring looks like," she said as she started walking off.

Confused, Ella ran to catch up with her.

"Jenny, wait up! Why are we going to find out what Phillip's mom's ring looks like?" she asked.

"Because," Jenny answered.

"Oh, because... Well, that just explains everything," Ella smarted.

"I knew it would once I told you," Jenny smarted back.

"Okay, seriously though, why?" Ella asked.

Jenny was quiet and kept walking.

"Jenny!" Ella snapped as she grabbed Jenny's arm to stop her.

"Ugh! Okay!" Jenny shouted. She lowered her voice and whispered in Ella's ear, "We're going to steal it back from the mermaids," and continued walking.

Ella had been listening very intently and, after hearing what Jenny said, stood there motionless hoping that she had heard wrong.

After a minute, Ella turned and ran after Jenny.

"Um, Jenny dear, I think I heard you wrong because it kind of sounded like you said we were... Ha-ha! That we were, ha! Ha-ha! Oh, gosh! That we were going to steal Phillip's mom's ring back from the, ha! From the mermaids! But I know you couldn't have said *that*! Ha... Right?" she was hysterical.

Jenny had stopped walking a ways back and was staring at Ella with concern while she had this...whatever it was Ella was having.

When Ella finally stopped her nervous and awkward laughter, Jenny just looked at her and said, "Right," and walked on.

Ella's shoulders dropped and with a sigh, she said, "That's what I thought," and ran to catch up with Jenny.

After walking around the ship for a while, checking rooms and corridors, Ella and Jenny found a man in the kitchen that they thought looked like a Phillip.

"Don't you think it's kind of wrong to try and find Phillip based on what we think he should look like because of his name?" Ella whispered.

"It's a long shot and yeah, a little wrong, but what's the worst that could happen?" Jenny asked. "Phillip?"

"Yes?" the man answered.

"You're Phillip?" Jenny asked.

"Yes, but did you ask that based solely upon my looks?" Phillip asked.

"Uh, maybe," Jenny replied awkwardly.

"That's wrong," he stated.

Jenny's face turned a little red, and Ella was trying to hide her giggles with her hand over her mouth.

"You know, I could be a Jim, or even a Frank," he mentioned. Ella lost it!

"You know, he makes a wonderful point, Jenny. He could be Frank, and we're over here thinking he's Phillip!" Ella stated, trying to stop laughing.

"I am Phillip, but I think it's terrible that you based your assumption solely on my looks!" he remarked.

Ella started laughing even harder. Jenny tried to hide her shame and embarrassment without much success in doing so.

"I'm sorry that I judged you solely on your looks, but we have something to ask you," Jenny stated with her face still red.

"Eh, forget it! I do look like a Phillip. I take it as a compliment! That means I look more important than just a deckhand," he winked.

Jenny managed to give a shy smile.

"Now, what do you need to ask me?" he asked.

"What does your mother's ring look like?" Ella asked.

"Give us every sort of detail possible!" Jenny told him.

"Oh, it's beautiful! The band on it doesn't look like a normal band. It has tiny gold leaves and rosebuds on it, and each of the rosebuds are tiny little rubies. And that's just the band! The top of the ring is surrounded by more gold leaves that are slightly bigger than the ones on the band and in the center, oh! In the center is a bright-red ruby! The brightest red you've ever seen! It's the most beautiful ring you'd ever see. Ah…" Phillip trailed off. He was obviously picturing the ring and more than likely picturing it on his bride.

Ella and Jenny looked at each other.

"We've got to get that ring back," they whispered together.

"There is no way a mermaid is going to give up a ring like that without a fight," Ella stated as she and Jenny were walking down the corridor.

"This is going to be a bit harder than I thought, but still doable," Jenny replied, trying to sound positive.

Ella gave her a look that said, *You're kidding, right?* But Jenny ignored her.

"Come on! Let's go tell Antonio so he'll stop being upset with us, mainly me. He likes you too much to stay mad for long," she stated with a slight grin.

Ella gave her a shove and rolled her eyes. Jenny laughed and just kept walking.

When Ella and Jenny got back to the main deck, they saw Antonio on the upper deck talking with some of the crew.

"Antonio doesn't look very happy. He actually looks kind of sad," Ella mentioned with a frown.

"Yeah, his crew probably isn't too happy about not going to get Phillip's ring. Especially after promising that he would," Jenny replied.

The two of them made their way to the upper deck where Antonio was at. When Toni saw Ella, he managed to shoot her a little smile. Ella gave a shy smile in return, and Jenny bumped her slightly.

"Captain, I think you ought to reconsider!" said the man Toni was talking to.

Toni had been semi-staring at Ella but returned to his conversation.

"There is nothing to reconsider. I will not put this entire ship and those aboard at risk!" Toni stated in a stern tone of voice.

"But, Captain—" the man started to say.

"Enough, Jeff. The people aboard this ship mean far more to me than gold!" Toni explained as he looked over at Ella. "My decision stands," he stated and waved Jeff off.

"So says the captain," Jeff replied with a sigh as he turned and walked away.

Antonio sighed. Jeff was the sixth man to ask him to reconsider his decision, and it was really starting to get him down. As the girls approached, they could see that Toni's face looked tired.

"What can I do for you, ladies?" Toni asked as he sat down on a crate.

"It's not what we can do for you. It's what *we* can do for you!" Ella replied.

Jenny looked at Ella as if saying, *Do you know what you just said?* And Toni raised his eyebrow. Ella smacked her forehead realizing what she had said.

"Ugh! I mean, it's not what you can do for us, it's what *we* can do for you," Ella corrected, turning a bit red from embarrassment.

Toni tried not to laugh.

"And what might that be?" he asked.

"We can get Phillip his mom's ring back," Jenny answered.

Toni had a surprised look on his face.

"Who told you?" he asked.

"We overheard some of the men talking about it, and we're sorry. We shouldn't have piped in before we knew the whole story," Jenny said.

"Can you forgive us?" Ella asked.

Toni looked from one to the other for a moment.

"Of course, I forgive you. I should've told you what was going on with the ring," he replied. "Can you both forgive me for not telling you?" he asked.

"Of course!" Ella answered.

"I'll think about it," Jenny winked. Toni rolled his eyes and smiled.

"If you can get that ring back, you'd really be helping me out. Phillip too. You'd make Phillip a very happy man. Not that much can make him unhappy right now with the thought of his girl always on the brain," he commented.

Ella and Jenny smiled.

"We'll get it back, and he can give it to her," Jenny assured him.

"How did the mermaids get it anyway?" Ella asked.

"Phillip wrote a letter to his mother telling her about the marriage and that if she blessed it, would she also come and see her son wed," Toni explained.

"So she died in a shipwreck coming here?" asked Ella and Jenny together loudly.

"No!" he semi-shouted. "Would you let me finish?"

Ella and Jenny fell silent, and Toni continued.

"Phillip's mother replied to his letter saying that she was unable to travel, but to show that she approved of the marriage, she would send the ring that his father had given her when they got married," he told them.

"And the cargo ship she sent it on sank on the way here," Ella finished the story, and Toni nodded.

"Okay, we're getting that ring back!" Jenny stated, sounding more determined than ever. Ella nodded in agreement.

Toni looked at both of them with careful thought in his eyes and said, "I can't let you."

Practically in shock by what they had just heard, they weren't exactly sure what to say. Jenny finally found her voice though.

"W-what do you mean you can't let us? What's that supposed to mean?" she asked.

Ella and Jenny waited for Toni's answer, feeling confused.

"You said it yourselves. A mermaid is not going to give up her treasure. Which means that you're either going to try to make a deal with them or you're going to try and trick them. Either way, you're putting yourselves in danger, and I can't knowingly allow that to happen. So I can't let you try and get the ring back," he answered so matter-of-factly that it annoyed Ella and Jenny.

As if he knew anything about our plan, Ella thought to herself, getting angry. *Not that we have the greatest plan in the world, but still!*

Jenny was about to say something, but Ella cut her off.

"We're going!" Ella stated in a stern tone with her arms crossed. Jenny nodded and crossed her arms as well.

Toni pushed his bangs out of his eyes and said, "No, you're not."

Ella glared at him.

He can't exactly stop us, she thought. *I mean, seriously, what's he going to do?*

Toni was trying so hard not to crack a smile or laugh at how cute he thought Ella was with her arms crossed, trying to stare him down. He cleared his throat.

"I said no, and that is my final word," he said as he stood up.

Ella hadn't realized how much taller Toni was than her up until that moment. Ella was still growing, but she was only about five foot four. Whereas Antonio looked to be about six foot.

Oh, so what? He's taller. Big deal! Ella laughed at her thought's joke. *Big deal,* she giggled rethinking it.

Ella suddenly realized that Jenny and Toni were staring at her while she randomly laughed, so she cleared her throat.

"And our final word is that we're getting that ring back! Come on, Jenny!" Ella said as she and Jenny walked away.

Toni thought seriously about what he should do next. Should he let them go, knowingly letting them walk into danger, or should he stop them and risk them not coming back to visit?

He started to run after them, but stopped himself. Although he knew he might regret it, he let them go.

"They'll be fine," he assured himself quietly as he watched them disappear to another part of the ship.

CHAPTER 4

The Power of Imagination

"Well, he didn't follow us," Jenny mentioned looking behind them.

"Good!" Ella said sharply.

"Whoa! You okay?" Jenny asked.

"I'm fine," Ella replied point blank.

"Okay..." Jenny said hesitantly.

Ella was quiet, but she looked like she might explode.

"Are you sure?" Jenny questioned.

"Ugh! Where does he get the nerve? The nerve to tell us what we can and cannot do! We can do whatever we want! You know, we could fly if we really wanted to!" Ella burst out, and Jenny laughed.

"Yeah, *I* know that, and we can fly later if you want. We'll visit Flora. Right now we have to get that ring though, so let's go with being mermaids," she said with a smile.

"You're right. Let's go!" Ella replied.

Ella and Jenny looked around to make sure that no one would see them.

"The coast is clear! Are you ready?" Jenny asked.

Ella nodded.

The two girls held hands and took one last look around before stepping over the edge of the ship and jumping into the water. Once the girls were in the water, they swam down instead of up, just in case someone had heard the splash. The girls were starting to run out of air though. Looking at each other, they shut their eyes for a brief second and imagined that they could breathe underwater.

"Ah!" Ella gasped as she let out the breath she had been holding.

"I know," Jenny replied, breathing hard. Both girls took a deep breath in.

"Okay, now we should imagine up some tails, would you agree?" Ella asked with a few bubbles escaping her mouth.

"Seems like the logical thing to do," Jenny answered.

The girls shut their eyes for a second and imagined that they had mermaid tails.

When Ella opened her eyes, she saw that Jenny had a pretty gold fish-colored tail. When Jenny opened her eyes, she saw that Ella was sporting a lovely emerald-colored tail.

"Nice tail!" they complimented in unison and then laughed.

"Let's go find some of our fellow mer-sisters," Jenny declared with a flick of her tail. Ella followed after her.

They had been swimming for about fifteen minutes when Ella commented, "Hey, I just had an idea."

"What's your idea?" Jenny asked.

"Why don't we just go to Mermaid Cove where the trade is supposed to be?" Ella asked sounding a little smart.

Jenny stopped midswim with a blank look on her face. After a few seconds of thinking, Jenny rolled her eyes and smacked herself on the forehead.

"Ugh! Why didn't I think of that?" Jenny asked, feeling silly.

Ella laughed.

"Well, come on then," she said as they started swimming in the direction they imagined Mermaid Cove would be.

After a while of swimming, something, or someone, zipped past them.

A bit startled, they stayed there completely motionless for a minute. As they cautiously started swimming again, they started to hear voices chattering. Ella and Jenny looked at each other and started swimming faster toward the voices. Finally, they came upon a clear and sunny cove with lots of coral, seaweed, fish and other sea life, and mermaids!

A couple of the mermaids swam over to greet Ella and Jenny.

"Hello and greetings, mer-sisters! I'm Coral," mermaid Coral greeted, sounding friendly.

"I'm Shelly. I've never seen you two around here before. Where are you from?" asked mermaid Shelly, being nosy.

"Oh yeah, we're from the South Atlantic sea. We heard about the thing here and that it was today. We thought that it sounded cool, so while we were traveling, we thought we'd stop by," Jenny replied, quite convincingly.

"Yep," Ella attested.

"I thought that all, except the North Pacific mermaids, were doing the trade scam? Why not just stay home?" Coral asked.

I knew it was a scam! Ella thought to herself.

"Yeah, that's where we're from, the North Pacific Sea," Jenny answered.

"You just said that you were from the South Atlantic though," Shelly pointed out.

"No, I meant that's where we've just *come* from. We've been traveling," Jenny corrected.

"Out of curiosity, why aren't you North Pacific mermaids doing the trade scam?" Shelly asked, sounding suspicious.

"I could think of a few different reasons, but I'm really not sure. As I said, we've been traveling," Jenny answered.

Man, she's good! Ella thought. Shelly started to say something, but Coral interrupted her.

"Oh, Shelly, stop being so nosy! Remember, we're all here for the same reason. To trick the humans and steal their treasures when their boats sink from hitting the coral shelf," Coral reminded her with a smile.

Ella and Jenny looked at each other; happy that they had stopped Antonio and everyone aboard his ship from coming here.

"So we told you our names, but we don't know yours," Coral mentioned.

"Oh! Silly us! I'm Jentle Wave with a J. I go by Jenny though," Jenny told her with a smile and looked at Ella.

"And I'm…" Ella had to think quickly. "Reefella! I go by Ella though," she smiled, happy she had thought of something.

"It's so nice to meet you fellow mer-sisters! Isn't it great that no matter which sea we're from that we all still call each other sisters? Unlike silly humans, all of us act like one big family! I just love it! I'm so happy that I'm not a human! I love being a mermaid!" Coral stated giddily.

Wow. She's a new kind of happy positive. It's kind of creepy, Ella thought to herself, trying not to appear freaked out.

"Oh, I know exactly what you mean," Jenny replied.

"Yeah, humans are so strange," Ella agreed.

"So, can we see the treasures you all brought to fool the humans?" Jenny asked, trying to sound casual.

"Sure! Come on! Oh, I want to show you my ring collection. I brought it just to show off!" Coral said with a wink.

Ella and Jenny followed Coral through the crowd to some rocks where there were lots of shiny human things. Mirrors and cups, swords and necklaces, bracelets and watches, compasses, a few books with gold writing on the covers, forks and knives, but strangely no spoons. There were a couple of scenery paintings and lots of gold coins. There were some gold and ivory brushes and combs and finally, assorted boxes made out of gold, coral, wood, rock, and clam shells with rings in them. Lots of rings!

Ella and Jenny were paying very close attention to every ring, looking for Phillip's mother's ring. Coral stopped and picked up a large, wouldn't you know it, coral box simply stuffed with perfectly placed rings.

"Here's my collection!" Coral beamed.

Jenny was still looking at the other boxes of rings, so Coral was mostly just showing Ella. Coral picked up one of her rings and held it up for Ella to see.

"This is my newest one! I found it in the oddest place. A cargo ship! Weird, huh? Isn't it beautiful though?" she asked.

Of course, Ella thought to herself, looking at Phillip's mother's ring as Coral held it. "Oh wow! That is beautiful, Coral! Jenny, you've got to see Coral's newest ring," she hinted.

"In a second," Jenny mumbled, so completely involved in her searching.

"Coral found it on a cargo ship! You *really* need to see this ring, Jenny!" Ella stated, hoping Jenny would get a clue. Sure enough, Jenny swam over.

"Isn't it beautiful?" she asked.

"It sure is! Could I hold it?" Jenny asked.

"Oh, I don't hand over any of my rings unless I'm trading for something better, and this ring would be pretty tough to beat!" Coral replied as she put the ring back in her box.

"So, you'd trade it if you could get something better?" Jenny asked.

"Of course! But it would have to be pretty impressive to top this one!" Coral stated.

"Could you excuse us for a wave? There's a watch over here that I want to show Ella," Jenny said.

"Sure! I think I'll go see if Shelly has traded anything yet," Coral answered as she swam off.

Once Coral was out of earshot, Jenny pretended to be showing Ella the watches.

"Okay, you've got to imagine that you have a more impressive ring than Phillip's mom's ring!" Jenny whispered.

"Wait a minute. If we're going to do that, then why didn't I just imagine that Phillip had his mom's ring back in the first place?" Ella asked.

"Because that would have been too easy and not as much fun as taking it from mermaids," Jenny answered.

"True, but imagining a replacement isn't really *taking* it," Ella remarked, using air quotes. "Isn't imagining a better ring too easy?" she asked.

Jenny opened her mouth to speak, but shut it again.

"Hmm… Good point," Jenny replied finally. "Okay, what's your plan then?" she asked.

Ella smiled.

"Just be ready to swim, fast!" she told her.

"Hey, everyone, here comes the first ship! Come on!" yelled a mermaid that had been sitting above the water on some rocks.

All the mermaids swam up to the surface to watch and give fake welcoming waves as the ship approached the coral shelf.

"Okay, when you see me jump out of the water, grab the ring and swim as fast as you possibly can away from here to where we left the ship. Got it?" Ella asked.

"Got it," Jenny answered. "Wait, why don't we just imagine that we're back on the ship?"

Ella and Jenny stared at each other for a second, smiled, and said together, "Too easy!"

Ella and Jenny swam up to the surface, and Jenny watched as Ella swam through the crowd and then disappeared under the water.

Ella got a little ways away from the other mermaids and closer to the ship before she popped her head out of the water yelling, "Stop! Turn back! There's a coral shelf, and you're going to hit it! Go back, it's a trap!"

Ella dove down and then jumped out of the water, giving Jenny her signal.

The other mermaids had started swimming after Ella to try and stop her, giving Jenny the perfect opportunity to dive down and grab Phillip's mom's ring.

Once Jenny grabbed the ring, she imagined a new one so Coral wouldn't be too upset and swam off as fast as her tail could propel her, which she was imagining to be pretty fast.

Ella was successful in warning the ship; it had just enough time to turn before it would've hit the coral shelf. With the mermaids starting to give up the chase, Ella was still swimming pretty fast, but she could breathe a little easier now. When the pursuit was finally over, Ella hid in some tall kelp to gather up enough strength to make it the rest of the way back to the ship.

"Phew! I thought they'd never give up. I'm exhausted!" Ella said, talking out loud to herself. "I seriously need to rest, or I'll never be able to make it back to the ship!"

Ella tucked herself under a big rocky shelf so she could be safely hidden inside the massive kelp forest and rest.

A good ways off in the distance, Jenny was almost to the ship. She could see it sailing along and used her last bit of energy to catch up with it.

"Almost there! Almost there! Come on tail, just a little bit farther!" Jenny encouraged her aching tail.

She was right by the ship now, but she didn't see Ella. Jenny assumed that if Ella's tail was as tired as her tail was, that she wouldn't want to trail the ship for miles waiting and just imagined that she was back on board. Jenny closed her eyes for a second and imagined that she didn't have a tail, and then she imagined that she was safely back on the ship with Phillip's ring.

Jenny opened her eyes and looked around for Ella. After a bit of searching, Jenny stood with her hands on her hips, puzzled.

Where is she? she thought. Jenny suddenly snapped her fingers.

"Antonio! Of course. That's where she must be!" she said to herself as she went to find him.

Jenny found Toni in his cabin logging stuff down in a journal at his desk.

When Jenny walked in through the open door, Toni looked up from his books with great relief on his face.

He looked behind Jenny, who was looking around the room.

"Where's Ella?" Toni and Jenny asked each other in unison.

They both got puzzled looks on their faces.

Toni stood up from his chair. He had a kind of stressed, freaking out, *now is when I regret letting them go*, mad sort of look on his face.

"What do you mean, where's Ella?" he asked, his voice getting a little louder. "She was with you!" he stated.

"Yeah, she *was* with me! *Was*, meaning past tense, meaning it already happened. Yes, she *was* with me, obviously not now though! I thought she would be with you by now!" Jenny semi-yelled.

"Why would she be with me? She was supposed to be with you! You both went to get the ring back!" Toni shouted.

"We got the ring back! That's why we split up! Ella was getting the mermaids to follow her while I grabbed the ring. She said to meet back here, so I figured she beat me and was with you!" Jenny shouted back.

*****

Meanwhile, Ella had gotten a good rest and was nearly to the ship.

"I know Jenny beat me by now. It took forever for my tail to stop being numb," Ella said to herself. "She and Antonio are probably having a great time with the crew or giving Phillip the ring. I bet everyone is so happy that we got the ring!"

Ella smiled as she thought about the happy faces that would await her.

*****

"You're not mad at me! You're mad at yourself, for letting us go! Of course, you really couldn't have stopped us and, man, Ella was mad at you for thinking you could!" Jenny laughed slightly.

Toni's face was red with frustration. He took a deep breath in and let it out. His face cooled, and Jenny could see the regret he had in his eyes.

After a long minute, he finally said, "You're right."

"What?" Jenny questioned.

"I said, you're right. I am mad at myself. Even though I knew I couldn't stop you guys, I could've tried harder," he told her. "If something happened to Ella—"

"What about Ella?" Ella asked as she came happily bouncing into the room.

"Ella!" Toni and Jenny yelled together.

CHAPTER 5

When Tomorrow Comes

"**M**an, not the faces I was expecting. You guys look terrible! Is the ring okay?" Ella asked with wide eyes.

Jenny ran over and gave Ella a hug.

"Hi," Ella laughed as she hugged Jenny back.

Antonio looked so relieved to see Ella; you'd think he might cry.

"So is the ring okay?" Ella asked again.

"Yes! It's right here," Jenny said as she handed Ella the ring.

Ella held up the ring and sauntered over to Toni.

"You didn't think we could do it. Well, ha! We got the ring back *and* saved you from having to replace your ship! What do you think of *that*?" she asked with a very pleased smile on her face.

Toni cleared his throat.

"I think that I owe you one. You saved my butt, and I'm sorry that I doubted you and Jenny. You're both amazing," he stated with a smile.

"And don't you forget it!" Ella demanded, beaming from ear to ear.

Toni rolled his eyes. Jenny absolutely loved this, and she couldn't help a few giggles.

"Come on. Let's go give Phillip his mom's ring!" Ella said as she bounced out of the room with Jenny following.

The whole ship gathered on the main deck while one of the crew members went to fetch Phillip.

"What's all this about, Captain?" Phillip asked when he entered the large crowd.

Toni smiled.

"It's been a great honor having you aboard, Phillip, but I believe this belongs to you," he stated as he handed Phillip the ring. "Now go marry that beautiful woman whose heart you've stolen!" he shouted.

"Yeah!" yelled the entire ship, including Ella and Jenny.

Phillip couldn't find the words. All he could do was smile as a few happy tears escaped from the corners of his eyes. Ella and Jenny felt so happy inside.

Toni looked over at Ella and Jenny, mostly Ella, and with a tip of his hat, he smiled and mouthed the words, *Thank you.*

Ella mouthed back, *You're welcome.*

Jenny gave Ella a little shove. She knew that smile wasn't for her; it was all for Ella. Ella's cheeks turned a little pink, and she shoved Jenny back.

With everything going on, Ella and Jenny hadn't noticed that it was starting to get dark.

"I better finish preparing dinner! Thank you, Captain!" Phillip finally managed to say.

Toni nodded with a smile.

As everyone went back to their duties, Toni walked over to where the girls were sitting.

"Well, fair maidens, you've saved the day! Will you do us the great pleasure of joining us for dinner?" he asked.

Ella and Jenny looked out at the setting sun and realized how late it was. Their faces saddened as they turned back to Toni.

"I wish we could, but we need to be heading home," Ella told him with that sad pain in her heart.

Toni nodded, trying to hide his disappointment.

"Well, I bid thee good night then, ladies!" he said as he bowed and kissed each girl's hand.

Ella blushed, but Jenny just rolled her eyes.

"Come on, Ella," she said as she pulled Ella by the arm.

"Good night, Antonio," Ella said with a smile.

"Will I see you tomorrow?" he asked.

"Perhaps," she answered vaguely.

*****

As Ella and Jenny opened their eyes, they saw that the street lights had already come on.

"Oh, man, we really better get inside!" Ella stated as she and Jenny stood up and made their way down the ladder.

"Perhaps," Jenny teased with an ornery grin on her face as she tried not to giggle.

Ella pushed her and grinned with embarrassment.

"You have a crush on your imagination, admit it!" Jenny laughed.

"Oh, like you have room to talk! Need I remind you of a certain fairy prince?" Ella asked.

"I only liked Prince Char because I had a crush on Charlie Conner at the time!" Jenny stated. "How is he by the way?" she asked after a minute, a bit red faced for a change.

"He's good. He asks how you are sometimes. Still, though, Prince Char was in your imagination, and you had a crush on him!" Ella pointed out.

"Yeah, but he was supposed to be Charlie, so my crush was based on a real person. I don't know anyone around here that looks like Antonio," Jenny countered.

"Me neither," Ella replied with a sigh.

Jenny looked at Ella, her tone had changed, and it sounded sad.

"I guess I'm just silly. I mean, to have a crush on someone I just thought up is pretty ridiculous. We should go on a different adventure tomorrow," Ella declared, hanging her head.

Jenny grabbed Ella's arm to stop her from going in the house.

"Hey, I was only teasing. It's okay if you imagine someone you like. Everyone does it," Jenny assured her in a caring tone.

"We can talk about it later...or never works too, whichever!" Ella stated as she pushed open the kitchen door.

Ella's parents were already at the table eating when the girls came in.

"Well, if it isn't the adventurers," Allan commented with a smile.

"We figured that you would come in soon, and we knew you two hadn't been on an adventure together for a while, so we thought we'd let you stay out a little longer," Emily told the girls.

"Thanks. Mom, can we talk a minute?" Ella asked. "Now?" she added.

Emily glanced at Allan, who gave a glance back. In parent language, this meant that something was up, but that one or the other would handle it and call if they needed backup.

"Of course, sweetie," Emily answered as she wiped her mouth and stood up. "Let's go in here."

"Will you tell me about the adventure, Jenny?" Allan asked. "I'm just itching to hear about it!"

Jenny smiled as she sat down to eat and tell Allan all about the adventure; just like she and Ella used to do.

Ella and Emily plopped onto the couch in the living room.

"What's up, sweetie?" Emily asked her daughter.

"Is it silly to have a crush on someone you just imagined?" Ella asked.

"Oh, is it Antonio?" Emily asked. Ella nodded, feeling a little embarrassed.

"No, sweetie, it's not silly. I think every girl has a fantasy guy. Do you want to hear something crazy though?" Emily asked.

Ella nodded.

"I married my fantasy guy!" Emily told her.

"You got married in your imagination?" Ella giggled.

"Oh yeah, lots of times! Here's the crazy part though," Emily whispered.

Ella listened intently.

"He's your daddy!" Emily stated.

"What?" Ella asked, looking utterly confused.

"Okay, before I ever met your daddy, before I ever knew he existed, he was my fantasy man. And I don't mean his personality, I mean him!" Emily explained.

"How? You must have…" Ella began.

"Nope! I never saw him a day in my life, and he had never been anywhere I had ever been in real life! Can you just imagine how far my mouth dropped open when I met him in person?" Emily laughed.

"I think I would have fainted!" Ella stated, joining in on the laughter.

"Now I don't know if Antonio is a real person, but God put daddy in my imagination, and I fell more in love with the real deal than I ever did with the one in my imagination. So, there is nothing wrong with having a crush on someone in your imagination. Just make sure that if Antonio never comes along in real life, that you'll let the man that God made for you steal your heart, because he's going to be the real deal," Emily assured her.

Ella smiled and hugged her mom.

"You'll think he's better looking too," Emily smarted, and the two of them burst out into a laughing fit.

"Thanks, Mom," Ella said, smiling.

"Anytime, my little sunshine," Emily replied.

When they got back to the kitchen, Jenny was to the part about Ella saving the unsuspecting ship and out swimming all the angry mermaids.

"What a rush! Did you make it back to the ship with the ring?" Allan asked.

"Of course, I did! Ella was nowhere to be seen though, so I thought she was already on the ship, but she wasn't!" Jenny stated, looking at Ella with fake anger.

Ella just shrugged her shoulders and kept eating.

"Since I didn't come back with Ella, Toni and I got into an argument, but it was over when Ella came in," Jenny told them.

"You guys got into an argument?" Ella asked. "Why?"

"We didn't know where you were, so we were worried. We disagreed on whose fault it was, but I won," Jenny answered.

"But it wasn't anyone's fault! Did you make Antonio feel bad, Jenny?" Ella asked.

"It's okay, he agreed with me," Jenny replied.

"Ugh! Jenny…" Ella began.

"Hey, it all worked out, and we saved the day, remember?" Jenny asked, ending the conversation.

After dinner, the girls went up to Ella's room to hang out and get ready for bed.

"Remind me before we leave in the morning to imagine my hair up. That way it doesn't whip across my face when we get to the ship, okay?" Jenny said.

"Who said that we were going to be on a ship tomorrow?" Ella asked shyly.

"Me," Jenny answered as she put her long blonde curls into a ponytail.

Ella smiled shyly. Jenny knew that Ella had done the same thing for her when she'd had that crush on the fairy prince, Char, so it was time for her to return the favor.

"So, I'm thinking that we get an early start, a little after dawn. Does that sound good?" she asked.

"No, that's too late. How about a little before dawn? Does that sound good?" Ella asked with a smile.

"Sound's good to me!" Jenny answered. "Good night, Ella!"

"Good night, Jenny," Ella replied.

Ella seemed to fall straight to sleep whereas Jenny laid awake, thinking.

"Where have I seen him?" Jenny asked herself quietly as she searched through her adventure memories with the image of Antonio.

After a while of thinking and searching, Jenny couldn't come up with anything from her adventure memories.

"Ugh!" she grunted as she rolled over and went to sleep.

*****

"Wake up! Wake up!" Ella demanded as she shook Jenny.

"Huh?" Jenny groaned.

"It's morning! Come on, we have an adventure to go on!" Ella stated.

"What time is it?" Jenny asked, rubbing her eyes.

"Four thirty. It's before dawn, but the sun will start coming up soon. So come on! Get up, get dressed, and let's go!" Ella said as she threw Jenny her clothes. "Hurry up!" she added as she left the room.

"Okay, I'm coming," Jenny replied as she got up.

After getting dressed, Jenny headed downstairs to meet Ella.

Ella was sitting at the kitchen table tapping her fingers impatiently while she waited for Jenny. Ella had written her parents a note explaining that they wanted to get an early start on their adventure and skipped breakfast.

"Okay, let's go!" Jenny declared as she entered the kitchen.

"Well, it took you long enough," Ella giggled as they headed out the kitchen door.

The girls climbed up the ladder to the platform and sat down. They then held hands and closed their eyes, imagining that they were on Antonio's ship.

When Ella and Jenny opened their eyes, they were surprised to see that they were on the docks of a port instead of Antonio's ship.

The port was abuzz with fishermen selling their catch, men unloading cargo ships, a few people haggling to get the best price for an item, and a lot of people walking around and everyone seemed to be yelling.

"Oof!" Ella blurted out as someone shoved past her, knocking her into Jenny.

"Oh, pardon me!" said the woman. "My apologies, I'm hardly paying any attention to my surroundings, and I didn't mean to bump into you."

"It's all right. You kind of expect to be bumped and shoved when you're on the docks of a port," Ella told the woman.

The woman smiled.

"I would really love to stay and chat, but I'm waiting for someone on a ship that's scheduled to come into port today. Please excuse me!" she said as she hurried off.

"Well, since we imagined ourselves on Antonio's ship and ended up on the docks, his ship must be here somewhere," Ella concluded as she looked around.

"Yeah. Let's go find it," Jenny said.

The girls weaved their way through the crowds, looking at ships while they searched for Antonio's.

"Hey, what's the name of Antonio's ship?" Jenny asked. "It might be a bit easier for me to find if I knew the name," she explained.

Ella stopped walking as she realized that she never did find out what Antonio had named his ship.

"I...I don't know," she stuttered. "I never found out!"

"How are we going to find Antonio's ship if we don't know the name of it?" Jenny asked. "We can't even inquire about it without the name!" she stated as she plopped down on a crate.

Ella plopped down next to her and sighed.

"We could walk to the end of the dock and see if anyone knows Antonio, I guess. That's the only thing I can think of to do," she admitted.

"Most people try not to associate with pirates, but it's worth a shot, right?" Jenny replied as she stood up.

As the girls got to the end of the docks, they saw the woman that had bumped into Ella.

"Do you think she's still waiting?" Ella asked.

"She probably wouldn't be standing there if she wasn't," Jenny answered.

"Good point. Let's start asking around," Ella suggested.

"Okay," Jenny agreed.

Ella and Jenny asked several people if they knew Captain Antonio Carter, and almost every person asked, "What's the name of his ship?"

"Ugh! You're right, Jenny. Without the name of the ship, we're sunk!" Ella declared.

"Don't give up hope yet. Let's ask those men unloading the cargo ship over there. They're more likely to associate with pirates," Jenny stated as she walked over with Ella. "Excuse us, but do you know the pirate captain, Antonio Carter?" she asked.

"What's the name of his ship?" asked one of the men.

"The Jewel of the Sea," answered a familiar voice.

Ella and Jenny whirled around to see the woman they had talked with earlier, the one that had bumped into Ella.

The woman walked over to Ella and Jenny; seeing their confusion, she said, "The captain you are looking for, Antonio Carter, captains *The Jewel of the Sea*."

"How do you know?" Ella asked, curiously.

"That's the ship I am waiting for. So I ought to know who captains it!" laughed the woman.

"You said that you were waiting for someone on a ship. Are you waiting for Antonio?" Jenny asked, skeptically.

"Ha-ha! No. I'm waiting for the cook on his ship. My fiancé, Phillip," the woman answered as she smiled. "My name is Caroline. It's a pleasure to meet you."

Ella and Jenny felt silly for not thinking of that first. They could see what Antonio meant when he told Phillip to "go marry that beautiful girl." Caroline really was beautiful. With her blue eyes and long curly red hair; no wonder Phillip was always thinking about her.

"My name is Jenny. We were so happy to hear about Phillip getting married. Congratulations by the way," Jenny said.

"Thank you! He's been on Captain Carter's ship for a few months now, but once they make port here today, Phillip and I are finally going to be together and get married!" Caroline told them.

Ella and Jenny could definitely see the excitement and happiness in her eyes when she talked about marrying Phillip.

"We're very happy for both of you," Ella stated, smiling.

"Thank you! So how do you ladies know Captain Carter?" Caroline asked.

"Oh, I knew Antonio when he was a cabin boy on Admiral Arnold Cloak's ship, *The Fair Maiden*," Ella answered.

"I just met him yesterday," Jenny stated.

"He went from a cabin boy to a pirate? Why?" Caroline asked.

Ella wasn't sure how to explain that one, and luckily, she didn't have to! About that time, Ella, Jenny, and Caroline could hear someone yelling. All three of them turned to see *The Jewel of the Sea* sailing into port and Phillip standing at the very front of the ship waving and shouting to his beloved. Caroline's face lit up like a firework as she waved to Phillip.

As the ship docked and the platform was set, Phillip ran off the ship and scooped Caroline up into his arms. Everyone on the ship started clapping and cheering when Phillip kissed her.

"All right, lads, this isn't the only reason we came to port. We need supplies, so get to work!" Toni shouted to his crew with a smile. As some of the crew left to fetch supplies, Ella and Jenny boarded the ship.

CHAPTER 6

Soon But Not Soon Enough

When Antonio saw the girls board the ship, he smiled; happy that they had come back.

"Good morning, ladies!" he greeted in a pleasant tone.

"Good morning, Captain!" Ella greeted with a smile.

"Good morning. So, what does the day hold, Captain Carter?" Jenny asked.

"You tell me," he replied.

"Hmm…" Jenny murmured as she looked up at the sky.

"I think that it's going to be a fair day. Good weather for sailing, and a rematch!" Ella remarked with a determined grin.

"A rematch?" Jenny echoed. "A rematch of what?"

"Ella has this strange idea in her head that she can beat me in a duel," Toni answered in a sarcastic tone.

Ella glared at him.

"Well, we never established a winner since you wouldn't accept the victory!" she stated.

"If you won, why didn't you accept the victory?" Jenny asked Toni.

"Because the way it happened isn't how I win. Nor is it how I allow anyone aboard my ship to declare victory either," he answered.

"What happened?" she asked.

Ella pulled up her sleeve to reveal the slash on her arm that she had received from Toni's blade.

Toni frowned, remembering the incident.

"It was just an accident. His blade moved one way, and I moved the wrong way!" Ella explained with a giggle, still remembering Toni's face.

Jenny examined Ella's slash mark for a few seconds before turning to Toni and saying, "I bet I could take you."

Ella smiled broadly.

"I bet she could too! She's better at swordplay than I am," she stated.

Toni rolled his eyes playfully.

"What do you say, Toni?" Jenny asked, feeling confident. "You and Ella have your rematch, and then you and I have a go."

Toni eyed back and forth between them for a minute, carefully considering the proposition.

"I have a better idea," he stated. "We'll fight separately, and then I'll fight both of you at once. Deal?"

Ella and Jenny looked at each other and then back at Toni.

"All right. Deal! If we win, we get bragging rights for beating the captain," Jenny declared.

"Fair enough," he responded.

As the crew returned to the ship with the supplies, everyone got ready to depart and get back out onto the open ocean.

Word had spread quickly about the duel between Ella, Jenny, and Toni, and the crew was getting anxious.

"Gather 'round, lads, we're going to have a duel!" Toni shouted to the crew.

Everyone quickly assembled and eagerly waited for the duel to start.

Ella was up first to fight Toni. As they stood on the main deck, she put up her blade and took her stance, ready to fight!

"Are you ready?" Toni asked.

Ella nodded.

Clank! Their blades clashed. *Cling!*

I wonder if he's just playing around with me again or if he's actually fighting? Ella thought to herself.

Just then, Toni's blade whizzed by her head.

Nope, he's fighting for real! she concluded.

After a few minutes, Toni finally took his opportunity to disarm Ella, sending her blade sliding across the deck.

"You're getting better!" Toni complimented, out of breath.

"Thanks," Ella said breathlessly as she bent over with her hands on her knees.

"Do you want a minute?" Jenny asked Toni as she came forward.

Toni shook his head.

"No, I'm fine," he answered as he took one more deep breath in.

"Are you ready?" he asked as he took his stance.

Jenny took her stance and nodded.

Even though Toni had just fought Ella, he showed no sign of it as he fought with Jenny.

Jenny was indeed a bit more skilled than Ella was, and the fight lasted a bit longer.

As Jenny tried to spin the sword out of Toni's hand, Toni got ahold of the weak part of Jenny's blade. He did an expulsion (a sharp scissor-like movement) and disarmed Jenny in an instant.

Jenny watched as her sword skidded across the deck like Ella's had.

The crew clapped and cheered as Toni defeated his second opponent.

Jenny was out of breath, but ready for more. Ella had gotten her second wind and was also ready to fight again. Toni was breathing harder than he was before though, and that concerned Ella.

If you've ever picked up an old-fashioned sword or saber at an antique mall or flea market, then you'd know that they are quite heavy. Even those who are skilled and practiced in the art of saber fencing eventually start to feel the real weight of the sword. Although disarming someone in fencing isn't cool and quite rude, when you have no protective padding to wear, a disarm dual is better than death. Also, unless you have been trained in the art of fencing, you should *never* pick up a sword with the thought that you know what you are doing.

Ella desperately wanted Toni to take a few minutes to rest before continuing, but he took a deep breath in and took his stance as he let it out.

"Antonio, why not rest a minute?" Ella asked sheepishly.

"Yeah, we should take a little break before we go again," Jenny agreed.

Toni nodded and sat down on a crate for a minute to catch his breath.

After everyone had a chance to rest, they were ready to continue. Ella, Jenny, and Toni all took their stances.

"Are we ready?" Ella asked.

Toni and Jenny nodded.

Cling! Clank! Clink! With every attack Ella made, Jenny followed and vice versa.

Man, he is *good!* Ella thought to herself. She was starting to get tired and couldn't believe that Toni was still fighting as well as he was.

About that time, Toni blocked Ella's attack, giving him enough time to catch Jenny's sword with an expulsion, knocking it out of her hand. As Ella attacked again, Toni got the weak part of Ella's sword; manipulating it, he spun it out of her hand and sent it sliding.

The crew cheered and shouted.

"Good fight, ladies!" Toni said, breathing heavily. "Jenny, if you hold your sword a little more firmly, it won't be so easy to knock it out of your hand with an expulsion."

"I'll try that next time. Thanks," Jenny replied, trying to catch her breath.

"All right, lads, shows over. Back to work," Toni ordered. He was still breathing quite heavily.

"Are you all right, Antonio?" Ella asked with a look of concern.

"Yeah, I'm fine. It's just been a while since I fought two at once. It's good practice though," he answered. "I better get back to work myself."

He grinned as he stared at Ella for a moment before walking off.

"So, what should we do?" Ella asked.

Jenny's stomach growled in response.

"I think we should get some lunch!" Jenny answered.

Just then, Ella's stomach also started to rumble.

"Sounds like a good plan! Should we eat here or go home?" she asked.

"Let's see," Jenny mumbled, looking at the sun in the sky. "I'd say it's a little past eleven thirty. Which means your mom would almost have lunch ready, and since we don't know what time they eat lunch here, I think we should go home and come back," she concluded.

"Alright. We'll go home, eat, and then come back. Let me go tell Antonio," Ella said as she went to find him.

Ella didn't have to look far. She found Toni on the upper deck of the ship talking with his first mate. Their conversation appeared to be important, so she stood there and waited patiently.

After a few minutes, the first mate noticed Ella standing there.

"Captain, I think the little miss would like a word," he said, pointing to Ella.

Toni turned around.

"What can I do for you, my lady?" he asked.

"I just wanted to tell you that Jenny and I are going to return home for lunch, but we'll be back afterward," she told him with a smile.

"Enjoy your lunch then. I'll see you soon," he said as he bowed.

Ella walked back down to the lower deck and found Jenny sitting on some crates.

"Finally. Are you ready?" she asked.

Ella nodded, and the two of them closed their eyes.

"Ella! Jenny! Lunch is ready! If you can hear me..." Emily yelled, trailing off.

"Coming!" they yelled together.

As Ella and Jenny climbed down the ladder, Ella suddenly stopped.

"What's wrong?" Jenny asked, staring up at her from the ground.

"Someone's moving into where Mr. and Mrs. Clarkson used to live," Ella answered, looking across the street a few houses down.

Jenny climbed back up the ladder to take a look. As Jenny was climbing back up the ladder, Ella started walking toward the house. All of a sudden, Jenny let out a gasp.

Ella turned around thinking that Jenny had slipped; seeing she that hadn't though, she asked, "What's wrong?"

Jenny shook her head and blinked, doing a double take at what she had just seen.

"Jenny, what's wrong?" Ella asked as she climbed back up to the platform.

"Nothing… I just thought I saw…" Jenny trailed off, shaking her head once again.

"What?" Ella asked.

"Never mind. I'm going insane!" Jenny stated as she jumped off the ladder.

Ella looked over at the new people moving in and then down at Jenny who was walking to the house. Confused, she jumped off the ladder and caught up with her.

"What do you think you saw?" she asked.

"Nothing, it's just my imagination lingering around and playing tricks on me," Jenny answered.

"Is the sea air getting to you?" Ella asked with a giggle.

"That, or malnourishment," Jenny smarted.

"Well, we better go eat then!" Ella stated as she opened the kitchen door.

The girls had almost finished eating when they heard a knock at the front door. Emily got up and went to answer it.

"Hey, Emily," greeted Jenny's dad, Rick. "Is Jenny ready to go?" he asked.

"Hey, Rick," Emily greeted. "They're just finishing up lunch. I think they were planning on going on another adventure though," she answered as she and Rick walked to the kitchen.

"Hey, sweetie, did you have fun? Hi, Ella," Rick greeted.

Ella's and Jenny's faces dropped like a ton of bricks. Rick couldn't be here to take Jenny away already!

"You're early," Jenny stated as she frowned.

"I told you I would be here by one," Rick responded.

"It's noon," Ella stated.

Rick looked at his watch.

"Alright. My bad. I'm sorry," Rick apologized.

"Dad, I never get to see Ella, and you're an hour early," Jenny fussed.

"Well, I think the news I have for you will make up for it. You and Ella will be able to see each other a lot more soon," Rick told them with a smile.

"How?" they asked together.

"The owners of the company I work for said that things have really fallen apart since I got transferred to Oklahoma and have decided to transfer me back here. So, that means—" Rick started to say.

"We're moving back!" Jenny yelled.

"You're moving back!" Ella yelled at the same time Jenny did.

Ella and Jenny jumped out of their chairs and started bouncing around the kitchen joyfully. They were far too excited to stay still.

"Remember though, it'll take us a while before we're ready to move back," Rick began. He then went down the list of everything that would have to be done and the timeframe he expected it would take. Needless to say, it absolutely killed the happy buzz.

Ella and Jenny sat back down at the table and rested their chins on their knuckles, feeling sad as they listened to Rick jabber on about the estimated three-month minimum he thought that it would take before they could move back to the little neighborhood outside of Rocheport.

By the time Rick was almost done laying everything out, it was two o'clock.

"Our adventure day is ruined! It's two o'clock," Ella whispered to Jenny, so softly that no one else would be able to hear.

"I know! We could've squeezed in at least five other adventures by this point," Jenny whispered back.

"Anyway, I just want you girls to get an idea of how soon this will all happen," Rick finally finished.

"Uh-huh," they grunted.

"Oh wow! It's two o'clock. Go and get your stuff, Jenny. We really need to get on the road," Rick stated.

Ella and Jenny got up from the table and slowly headed upstairs to Ella's room to get Jenny's overnight bag.

"I didn't hear anything that remotely even resembled *soon*!" Ella stated as they got to her room.

"Yeah. It all sounded *long* to me," Jenny agreed as she stuffed her pillow into her bag.

Both girls flopped onto Ella's bed and sighed.

"I'm sorry that I can't go back to the ship with you," Jenny said after a minute.

"It's okay," Ella replied. "You know, even though it's going to take a while, I'm happy that you're moving back."

"Me too," Jenny replied, smiling.

The girls laid on Ella's bed staring up at the glow-in-the-dark stars she had on her ceiling until Rick called that it was time to go.

Ella and Jenny sluggishly made their way downstairs and said their goodbyes.

"I promise that I'll pack faster than a rat," Jenny stated as she and Ella hugged.

"Every time you walk past something, just throw it in a random box. That'll make it go faster," Ella told her.

They laughed, but tears soon ran down their cheeks.

With one last hug at the car, Ella and Jenny waved to each other as the car pulled out of the driveway and drove away.

Emily put a comforting arm around Ella and kissed her daughter's head.

Everything will go back to the way it used to be...soon, Ella thought, hugging her mom as the last of her tears fell.

"Can I go for a walk?" she asked.

"Sure, but what about your adventure?" Emily asked.

"I just want to clear my head first," Ella replied as she started walking.

Ella walked around the neighborhood at least twice before she headed for home.

On her way, she ran into Mrs. Matthews, who was welcoming the new people moving into the neighborhood.

"Hi, Mrs. Matthews," Ella greeted as she was passing by.

"Hello! Oh! Ruthella, this is Mrs. Carter! She and her husband, Tony, and their sons have just moved here from Oklahoma!" Mrs. Matthews told her.

Ella stopped and gave a polite wave.

"Please, call me Mariah," Mariah said. "I'm so sorry. I've already forgotten your name."

"Ruthella, but everyone calls me Ella," Ella replied, not feeling very social at the moment.

"How old are you, Ella?" Mariah asked. "I'm asking because I have three boys that don't know anyone yet."

"Thirteen," Ella answered.

"Ruthella is a very sweet young lady! Her and her friend Jennifer always used to rake my yard for my husband and I in the fall," Mrs. Matthews mentioned. "Jennifer moved away a few years ago, though. So now it's just Ruthella."

"Jenny is moving back soon," Ella told her, hoping that the more she said soon, the *sooner* it would actually be.

"I'm sure my sons would be willing to help with leaf raking this fall. They're actually around your age, Ella. My youngest, Mark, is twelve. My middle child, Anton, just turned fifteen. And my oldest, Chris, will be seventeen next month," Mariah explained as she talked with her hands.

"I'd love to meet them and show them around the neighborhood, but perhaps some other time. It was nice meeting you," Ella said as she headed for home.

Ella knocked on the back door twice so her mother would know that she was home but staying outside.

She climbed up the ladder to her platform, leaned back against the tree trunk, and sighed. Going on adventures was a lot more fun when you had someone to go with you.

"I've gone on adventures by myself since Jenny moved away," she told herself. "It won't be forever. Soon Jenny will move back, and it'll be just like it was this weekend, just like it was before she moved."

Ella smiled as she sat down. She sat there for a minute staring up at the gray clouds that had formed while she was on her walk and then closed her eyes.

CHAPTER 7

Walk the Plank

Instead of imagining herself somewhere on an adventure, Ella just wanted to remember some of the adventures she had gone on before. She remembered the time that she and Jenny had gone to London, England, and found the queen's missing ruby necklace and both received a ladyship. She remembered the time that she and Jenny had with some leprechauns that were trying to find a good place to hide their gold instead of at the end of rainbows. She remembered seeing the fairy princess, Flora, be crowned queen and the crush that Jenny had on Prince Char. She remembered riding horses through the old west trying to catch a robber and seeing wild mustangs run free. She remembered when the Master of Arms had first taught her and Jenny how to sword fight and how hard Jenny practiced. She also remembered the last time she was on the admiral's ship, *The Fair Maiden,* and when she had first met Antonio as a cabin boy.

Ella opened her eyes, thinking about how Antonio had become a great pirate captain that his crew respected.

She closed her eyes again, this time imagining that she was on Antonio's ship, *The Jewel of the Sea.*

BOOM!

Ella opened her eyes, startled by the sound of cannons being fired.

BOOM!

The Jewel of the Sea was in a battle with another ship! Ella looked around; everyone was running all over the place, gathering swords and cannonballs to fight the other ship. She could see an island nearby where she suspected the other ship had come from. Clearly, they weren't too keen on pirates.

BOOM!

Another cannon went off. Ella wasn't exactly sure what she should do other than try and stay out of everyone's way. All of a sudden, there was a hand over Ella's mouth as she was being dragged away.

"Am I being taken hostage?" she asked herself as she wiggled.

"Stop moving! It won't do you any good!" shouted the man that was taking Ella.

Oh really? Ella thought.

She bit the hand that was covering her mouth and let out a high-pitched scream as she started to run. The man grabbed Ella's arm, so Ella punched him in the nose and kicked him in the shin.

The Jewel of the Sea had just taken victory by sinking the ship it was fighting.

The man had released her after she kicked him, and as she was running to make her escape, she tripped over some rope and fell.

"Oof!" she blurted out as she hit the deck.

When she tried to get up, she fell back down because her foot had gotten tangled in the rope that she tripped over and was stuck!

The man that had tried to kidnap her approached and drew his sword. Ella's eyes were wide as she saw the blade coming down upon her.

Cling!

Toni blocked the man's sword with his own and disarmed him in an instant!

"You have two choices: you can walk the plank with all your friends and swim back to your island, or..." Toni shrugged his shoulders, his blade to the man's neck.

The man gulped.

"That's what I thought," Toni commented.

He led the man over to the plank, and the man jumped into the water. The whole ship was cheering over their victory.

Ella had finally gotten herself free from the entanglement of rope and walked over to Toni.

"Are you alright?" he asked as he put his hand on Ella's shoulder.

"Yes, thanks to you! I had no idea you could disarm someone that fast!" she stated. "You really have been taking it easy on me, haven't you?" she asked.

An ornery smile came to Toni's face, and he shrugged his shoulders. Ella rolled her eyes.

"I'll take that as a yes!" she replied, making Toni laugh.

"Like I said before. You're good, but you're not *that* good yet," he countered.

"No kidding," she remarked. "So, why were you fighting with that other ship?" she asked.

"We crossed over into their waters, and this island has a ban on pirates," he answered. "So we fight or get killed."

"Why do they have a ban on pirates?" she asked.

"I don't know. Some islands are just like that," he answered.

"Captain, the ship has sustained no real damage. A few broken windows are all she endured," the first mate told Toni as he came over.

"Thank you, Vince. Are we out of enemy waters?" Toni asked.

"Yes, Captain! Shall I set a course for the nearest port?" Vince asked.

"Yes. We'll need to repair the ship as soon as possible," Toni answered.

"Aye, aye, Captain!" Vince said as he walked away.

Toni turned his attention back to Ella.

"That was a very long lunch. Where's Jenny?" he asked.

Ella's eyes grew wide.

"You mean she's not here?" she asked, being dramatic. "She must've been captured!"

"What!" Toni shouted as he started for the upper deck.

"Antonio!" Ella yelled, trying to stop him. "Antonio! I was kidding!"

Toni stopped and turned around.

"Jenny didn't get captured?" he asked in a serious tone.

"No, she just went home," she answered. "Sorry, I didn't know you would freak out."

"Please don't joke about stuff like that. The people aboard my ship mean far more to me than gold," he stated.

"Sorry," she responded, feeling guilty.

Toni grinned and playfully pushed her.

"Just don't let it happen again," he said.

Ella smiled and pushed him back.

"Better watch it, that's the arm that got cut," she stated.

"Oh, sorry," he said, frowning.

While Toni went to attend to some business, Ella walked over to the side of the ship and looked out onto the horizon, admiring the beautiful colors of the setting sun.

"Wait a minute. Sunset!" she muttered as she ran off to find Toni.

"Whoa, where's the fire?" Toni asked as Ella ran up to him.

"No fire. I have to go," she answered.

"Go where?" he asked, looking disappointed.

"I have to go home, the sun is setting," she answered pointing to the sky.

"Will I see you tomorrow?" he asked.

"I'll be here after school," she answered.

Toni nodded, took Ella's hand, and kissed it.

"Good night, Lady Ella," he said as he bowed.

"Good night, Captain Carter," she said as she walked off; her cheeks red.

Back on the main deck, Ella sat down on some crates and closed her eyes.

She sat there for a minute after opening her eyes, looking at how much darker the clouds had gotten. She could also hear some thunder off in the distance; a storm was definitely coming.

"I hope it's not raining while I wait for the bus in the morning," she mumbled to herself, climbing down the ladder.

"There's my girl! I heard the good news about Jenny moving back," Allan mentioned when Ella came through the backdoor.

"Hi, Daddy. Yeah, she'll be back soon," Ella replied, using the word *soon* again.

"So, how was your adventure?" he asked.

"It was good. Antonio saved me from being captured by people from an island that has ban on pirates. I'm really tired now. Can I skip dinner and just go to bed?" she asked.

Emily and Allan looked at each other.

"Sure, sweetie. Is everything okay though?" Emily asked.

"Yeah. It's just been a long day, and I miss Jenny," Ella answered.

As soon as she got up to her room, she changed, flopped on her bed, and fell fast asleep.

CHAPTER 8

Unexpected Surprises

*B*eep! *Beep! Beep!* Ella's alarm clock started going off, reminding her that it was a school day.

"Ugh!" she grunted, hitting the clock's off button.

Ella got out of bed and looked out her bedroom window to see pouring rain.

"That'll make waiting for the bus more fun," she remarked sarcastically to herself.

By the time Ella left the house to go wait for the bus though, the rain had stopped.

"Hey, Ella," said Chip Daniels when Ella got to the corner.

"Hi, Chip," Ella greeted.

"Sorry about the eraser the other day," he apologized.

"It's okay. I knew you were probably aiming for Charlie," she replied.

"I was. Did you meet the new kids yet?" he asked. "They just moved into the Clarkson house," he said, pointing to the house across the street.

"I met their mom, but I haven't met them yet," she answered.

Before Jenny moved away, the only three kids around Ella's age that lived in her neighborhood were Jenny, Chip, and Charlie Conner. Although Ella considered Chip and Charlie to be her friends and talked to them, they didn't hang out with her or Jenny very often.

"Mark is going to be in our class, so you'll get to meet him today. Anton and Chris are in high school though," Chip explained. "Ouch!" he shouted, holding the back of his head.

When Chip and Ella turned around, they saw Charlie walking up, and he had successfully hit Chip in the head with an acorn.

Chip threw the acorn back, but Charlie dodged it. So Chip put Charlie in a headlock; not an uncommon occurrence for the two of them.

"Hi, Charlie," Ella greeted, moving a few steps over.

"Hi, Ella!" Charlie greeted as he shoved Chip off.

A few minutes later, the bus pulled up to the corner and opened the door to let Ella, Chip, and Charlie on.

"What about the new kids?" Ella asked.

"What new kids?" Charlie asked. "You mean Mark, Anton, and Chris?"

"Yeah," Ella answered as she sat down.

"They said that their dad was taking them to school this morning, but that they'd be riding the bus home," Chip explained as he plopped down across from Ella and Charlie.

"Yeah, but Anton and Chris would be on a different bus, remember?" Charlie asked.

"You know what I meant!" Chip retorted.

Ella rolled her eyes; it got kind of annoying hearing Charlie and Chip bicker sometimes.

At school

"Good morning, young adults!" the teacher, Mrs. Dean, greeted when everyone was seated.

"Good morning, Mrs. Dean," the class replied.

"We have a new student joining us today. Would you please come up and tell us a little bit about yourself?" Mrs. Dean asked.

Ella watched as a boy with short sandy blond hair stood up and confidently walked to the front of the room.

"Thank you, Mrs. Dean! Hello, everyone, my name is Markel, but I generally go by Mark. Although if you *really* wanted to get my attention, just do what my parents do and yell Markel James!" Mark smarted as everyone laughed. "I'm only twelve, so I'm probably the youngest one in this class, am I right?" he asked as he looked over at Mrs. Dean, who nodded. "I just moved here from Oklahoma with my parents and my two older brothers, Antonio and Christopher,"

Ella's heart jumped when she heard Mark say that his brother's name was *Antonio*.

"I like reading, the great outdoors, video games, and orange slices on my pizza!" he told them.

The entire class made a sound of utter disgust.

"Hey, don't knock it until you've tried it! Anyway, I look forward to meeting and getting to know each and every one of you in the days and hours to come! Mrs. Dean, thank you for letting me have this moment in the spotlight, but now it's your time to shine. Take it away!" Mark said as he took a bow and returned to his seat.

"Thank you, Markel. Alright young adults, now I know you were responsible and remembered to do your homework over the weekend," Mrs. Dean said, eyeing her students.

"Antonio? I thought his brother's name was Anton?" Ella whispered to Charlie, who sat in front of her.

"No, his name is Antonio, but he goes by Anton because he and his dad have the same name," Charlie whispered back.

"Hmm…" she mumbled.

When the lunch bell rang, Ella jumped out of her chair and walked over to Mark's desk.

"Hi, Mark! We haven't met yet, but I live a few houses across the street from you. I'm Ella," she introduced herself.

"Hi, Ella! It's really great to meet you!" Mark said as he shook Ella's hand. "Are you by chance friends with Chip and Charlie? Because I remember someone saying something about a girl named Ella…" he trailed off as if trying to recall the memory more clearly.

"Yeah, I am. So, you said you have two brothers?" she asked, trying to sound casual.

"Yeah, Anton and Chris," he answered. "I'll introduce you to them after school. Chris for sure anyway! I don't know if you'll get to meet Anton right away though."

"Why?" she asked.

"He does fencing. You know, sword fighting? He wanted to see if his school had like a fencing club or something that he could join. So he might not be home right away," he explained.

"He does sword fighting?" she asked.

"Yeah, he's really good!" he answered. "He actually set a record at the fencing club he was part of back in Oklahoma for having the fastest disarm!"

"Wow! That's impressive! We should probably get to lunch. Do you want to sit together?" she asked.

"I would love to!" he answered.

It was nice to have someone to sit with at lunch for a change. Since Jenny had moved away, Ella was usually by herself.

"You know, I really only had one friend in Oklahoma, but we never hung out other than at school. Since you live right down the road, maybe we can be friends outside of school?" Mark asked with a hopeful smile.

"I would like that," Ella replied, smiling.

"Really?" he asked.

"Yeah!" she answered.

Mark smiled brightly.

"Nobody at my old school really talked to me. To them, I was the weird, chatty kid that can't run," he told her.

"Well, I definitely don't think you're weird. The orange slices on pizza thing sounds gross though," she mentioned.

"Again, don't knock it until you've tried it!" he said with a laugh. "After that, if you don't like it, you can join my brothers and everyone else with their immense dislike for it."

Ella laughed.

"I guess it's only fair," she stated.

"Exactly!" he replied. "So you know a little bit about me, but I don't really know anything about you," he mentioned after a minute.

"What do you want to know?" she asked.

"The basics, I guess. Favorite color. What you like to do outside of school. If you have any pets. How old you are. Stuff like that," he answered.

"Okay. Well, my favorite color is red. I like reading and going on adventures. I don't have any pets, and I'm thirteen," she told him.

"Cool! So you're a year older than me. What kind of adventures do you go on?" he asked, curiously.

Ella smiled.

"I go on adventures in my imagination," she answered.

A look of pure excitement came to Mark's face.

"Anton and I do that too!" he exclaimed.

That strange thought crossed Ella's mind once again, but she pushed it aside.

"Really?" she questioned. "Do you go on adventures together?"

"Usually, but not lately," he answered.

"Why?" she asked.

"We've just been busy moving, and I haven't felt like adventuring," he answered.

"Does Anton ever go on adventures without you?" she asked, trying to sound as casual as she possibly could.

"Yeah. I go on adventures without him too. Why?" he asked.

"Just curious," she answered.

The rest of the school day went by in a fog to Ella as she thought about crazy possibilities.

No, it just has to be one of those freaky coincidences! she thought to herself on the bus ride home. *But what if... No! It's just a freaky coincidence, because there is no way!*

The bus stopped at its usual street corner and let Ella, Chip, Charlie, and Mark off.

"Mark, do you want to come over later and play video games with me and Chip?" Charlie asked.

"I wish I could, but I have a lot of unpacking to do. Thanks for the offer though," Mark replied.

"Okay. See you guys tomorrow," Charlie said as he and Chip started walking home.

As their bus drove away, another bus pulled up to the corner and opened its doors, letting off two older boys.

One of the boys was a little taller than the other, with spiked dark-brown hair and muscular arms. The other boy had the hood of his jacket up though, so Ella couldn't get a good look at him. Mark hurriedly walked over and hugged both of them.

That must be Chris and Anton, she thought as she walked over.

"How was your first day, little brother?" asked the taller boy.

"It was good! Chris, Anton, this is Ella, she's in my class and lives over there," Mark told them, pointing. "Ella, these are my brothers, Chris and Anton!"

Ella waved, feeling a bit shy for once.

Anton suddenly pushed off his hood as if he could no longer see or if he didn't believe what he saw, and his eyes grew wide for a moment.

When Ella could finally see his face, her jaw almost hit the ground. Standing right in front of her was Antonio! Antonio whom she had met as a cabin boy. Antonio that was now a pirate captain. Antonio that was standing in front of her in the real world instead of in her imagination!

"Ella, are you okay?" Mark asked.

Ella was completely speechless! This was different than when she found out that Antonio had gone from cabin boy to pirate captain. It was different because that was all in her imagination, and this was the real world.

"Ella?" Mark questioned.

"Guys, can I have a minute alone with Ella?" Antonio asked.

"Sure. Maybe you can get her to talk," Mark answered.

"Good luck, bro!" Chris said with a grin as he patted Antonio on the shoulder.

Antonio rolled his eyes and pushed his brothers toward their new house. He took a deep breath as he turned back to Ella and stood with his hands in his jacket pockets, waiting for her to come out of shock.

"Okay, I'm going out on a limb here, but I'm judging by the look on your face that this is a bit surprising?" he asked. "I know that I'm personally a little surprised, but probably a lot less than you are."

A bit surprising? A bit surprising is when a movie theater runs out of popcorn. A bit surprising is when the wind blows a leaf in your face. A bit surprising is when you find five dollars in your pocket that you didn't know was there. No, a bit surprising couldn't even begin to describe how Ella was feeling. She was in utter shock!

CHAPTER 9

Imagination or Reality

"Ella, can you speak?" Antonio asked.

"I need to sit down!" she stated, sitting down on the sidewalk.

Antonio sat down beside her.

"This kind of reminds me of when you found out that I was a pirate, because you couldn't speak at first then either," he joked.

"That was different! That was just in my imagination!" she exclaimed. "This is real!"

"What if it wasn't just in your imagination?" he asked.

"What do you mean?" she questioned.

"The people, the mermaids, the sword fights, everything you've ever imagined—what if it was all real?" he asked.

"If it was all real, then it wouldn't be your imagination. It would be reality," she answered.

"And that would mean that everything you imagine is real," he replied.

Ella gave him an unconvinced look.

"You don't believe me. I can see it on your face," he said.

"Would you believe you?" she asked.

"I didn't believe it at first either. In my mind, I had to have some sort of proof to be convinced of something that intense! But if it wasn't real or somehow shared, then how else would I know that we

78

met when I was a cabin boy on the admiral's ship, *The Fair Maiden*?" he asked.

Ella's eyes grew wide and her mouth dropped open again.

Antonio laughed.

"Didn't you ever think about how you actually got your homework done if you just imagined that you did it?" he asked.

Ella couldn't answer him; she really *hadn't* ever thought about it before and now felt very silly.

"No, it's impossible!" she stated.

"Ahem…" he coughed, gesturing to himself.

Ella's head was busier than the highway during rush hour; this was a lot to take in.

"I need time to think about all of this. I'm not fully sure that I'm not just imagining all of this somehow," she said. "Can we talk tomorrow?" she asked.

"As you wish, my lady," he answered, standing up and helping Ella to her feet.

"Thank you," she said and started walking home.

Antonio watched her for a minute, wondering what might be going through her head, and then walked home.

Ella got home and went straight to her room without saying a word. She was laying on her bed thinking and staring up at her glow-in-the-dark stars when a knock on her door interrupted her.

"Come in," she called, sitting up.

"Hey. How's my girl?" Allan asked.

"Hi, Daddy. I'm okay. I'm just having a hard time believing something right now," she told him.

"Anything I can help with?" he asked, sitting down on Ella's bed.

"Maybe. Do you think that the things we imagine could be real?" she asked.

"How so?" he asked.

"Like my adventures. The places I go and the people I meet. Do you think that it could all somehow be real?" she asked.

"I think that your imagination is powerful enough to take you anywhere. Whether that place is real or not is for you to decide," he stated.

Ella sighed; that wasn't exactly the answer she was hoping for.

"Did I ever tell you the story of how I met your mommy?" he asked.

Ella shook her head.

"You're going to think that I'm crazy, but I actually met your mommy when I was helping Sherlock Holmes solve a case," he began.

"What? How is that even possible?" she asked, giving him a very confused look. "Sherlock Holmes is a storybook character," she stated.

"You don't just get that imagination of yours from your mommy, you know! I was quite the adventurer myself. There she was, spinning her red umbrella as she walked along the street. I swear, I think my heart skipped a beat when I saw her! She was the most beautiful girl I had ever seen in my life! After getting to know her, I told myself that if I ever found a girl like her in the real world, I would marry her. It was definitely a surprise when I actually met your mommy outside of my imagination!" he told her. "And it was an even bigger surprise to find out that your mommy also knew me in *her* imagination!"

Ella remembered the story that her mom had told her; the story about Allan being the guy that she thought she had imagined, but turned out to be real.

"My imagination turned into a reality when I met your mommy; and who's to say that imagination isn't just a reality that we've yet to discover?" he asked.

"Let's say that I did happen to discover one of those realities, but I found it hard to believe?" she asked.

"Well, I could tell you that I saw a bowl of flying oatmeal the other day, and you would probably find that hard to believe, but you could choose to believe me even if I couldn't provide you with any proof of said flying oatmeal," he answered with a laugh.

Ella laughed thinking about what a bowl with wings coming out of it would look like.

"What if I had proof standing right in front of me though, and it was still a bit much for me to believe?" she asked.

"Everyone requires their own idea of proof before they can believe something. Maybe the proof you have now isn't the proof you require," he answered.

"But what if everything that I imagine on my adventures is somehow the real world?" she asked.

"Then living life is your greatest adventure of all!" he answered and kissed Ella's head.

Ella smiled and gave her dad a hug.

"I love you, Daddy!" she said.

"I love you too!" he replied.

"Hey. Dinner's ready if anyone's hungry," Emily said, coming into the room. "Is everything okay?" she asked.

"Everything is good for me. How about for you, Ella?" Allan asked.

"Everything is great!" Ella answered, smiling.

CHAPTER 10

It's All Real

The next morning promised to be one of the last hot days of August with temperatures in the low eighties. So instead of putting on a T-shirt and jeans, Ella put on a tank top and a pair of shorts and went downstairs for breakfast.

"Good morning, little sunshine, are you ready for school?" Emily asked as she was cooking some bacon.

"Yeah. I'm glad it's going to be hot today. I was starting to get sick of all the rain," Ella replied.

"Yeah. Rain is good, but there's only so much of it you can stand until you're bored with it," Emily commented, giving Ella a plate of food.

"Yeah," Ella agreed.

"Goodness! How did you get that?" Emily asked, pointing to Ella's arm.

Ella was confused until she looked at her arm, and then her eyes grew wide. There on her arm was the slash mark from Toni's sword that she had gotten the first time that they had fought.

"It really happened," she whispered to herself.

"What did you say?" Emily asked.

"I'll tell you about it later! I have to go!" Ella said, grabbing her backpack and rushing out of the house.

Ella ran down the block as fast as she could to the corner where everyone was waiting for the bus.

"Antonio!" she yelled.

Antonio looked up to see Ella running toward him.

"Whoa, where's the fire?" he asked.

"No fire. Look!" she said panting and pointing to the mark on her arm.

Antonio examined the mark very closely for a minute and then smiled.

"It's all real," she whispered to Antonio, who nodded.

"How'd you get that, Ella?" Mark asked, being nosy, as he and the other boys came over.

"I did it," Antonio answered.

All the boys looked at him with astonishment, especially Chris and Mark.

"Anton—" Chris began in an older brother tone of voice.

"It was an accident!" Ella chimed in.

Chris raised his eyebrow at Antonio, who nodded.

"Okay," Chris said.

"How?" Mark asked, staring at the scar.

"You ask a lot of questions sometimes, little brother," Antonio commented.

Mark crossed his arms and waited.

Antonio playfully rolled his eyes and bent down to whisper in his little brother's ear.

"Oh!" Mark exclaimed.

Ella looked at them suspiciously.

"Remember yesterday when I told you that someone had told me about a girl named Ella?" Mark asked.

Ella nodded.

"It wasn't Chip and Charlie," Mark stated.

Ella looked at Antonio, who shrugged his shoulders and smiled.

About that time, the high school bus pulled up to the curb to pick up Chris and Antonio.

"See you after school?" Antonio asked Ella.

Ella smiled shyly and nodded.

"Until then, my lady," he said as he bowed and got on the bus.

Pulling up behind the departing high school bus, the seventh-grade bus opened its doors.

As Ella sat looking out the window, she smiled to herself, knowing one thing for sure—imagination would never die. For within all who imagine is the ability to go *off on an adventure*.

And *that* is when you truly discover *it's all real*.

ABOUT THE AUTHOR

D.M.Rose grew up on a farm near a small historical river town. In her childhood years, she spent her mornings doing homeschool lessons and her afternoons exploring the woods, the creek, and the rest of the farm that her family lives on. Much like Ella, the main character in her book series, she spent countless hours in her favorite tree, thinking, dreaming, and imagining. This real-life tree also has a platform built onto it, making a comfortable place to take in the scenic areas of the farm, breathe in sweet-smelling fresh air, and enjoy watching her horses roam the pastures.

She was inspired to write her first book series to encourage imagination and the spirit of adventuring outdoors. Her books feature strong family values and positive role models who rely on God and each other to solve the challenges that they face.

CPSIA information can be obtained
at www.ICGtesting.com
Printed in the USA
LVHW031450261120
672639LV00004B/408